Sparkles of Discontent

Robert Tucker

BookLocker

Published by BookLocker.com, Inc., St. Petersburg, Florida.

Library of Congress Cataloging in Publication Data
Tucker, Robert
Sparkles of Discontent by Robert Tucker
FICTION / Mystery & Detective / Women Sleuths | FICTION / Thrillers / Crime | FICTION / General
Library of Congress Control Number: 2019911580

Printed on acid-free paper.

Booklocker.com, Inc.
2019

First Edition

Dedication

This book is dedicated to Emily, Michael, and especially Nancy, who puts up with me every day and still loves me.

Part 1: Diamond Dreams

Chapter 1

"The door was wide open, wood splintered. The room smelled like fish gone bad and gunpowder." *That acrid smell always reminds me of the Fourth of July.* Detective Nia D'Amato stopped, staring at a Mondrian print hanging behind the department's psychologist.

Doctor Mary Alice Young finished jotting a note and looked up over her glasses. "Please continue, detective."

"Someone was crying from behind a sofa on the other side of the living room. I released the catch and drew my gun, stepping over broken stuff scattered across the carpet. I stopped and leaned over the sofa. A woman was crouched over the body of a man covered in blood. She looked up, startled. I could hear muffled sounds of someone cursing and things crashing to the floor. I pressed a finger to my lips and walked quietly down a hallway. I stopped just outside an open door. A man with his back to me, was pulling open drawers and tossing things behind him. I identified myself and ordered him to freeze and put his hands into the air. He stopped. I heard him mutter, *fucking cops.* I saw one arm move in front of him. Then he slowly put his arms out and wheeled around all of a sudden. He fired one shot. I returned fire, hitting him in the chest." She looked down, staring at the bullet-riddled body of the dead man.

The doctor looked back through her notes. "And you stated you shot him, three times. Is that correct?"

"Yes."

"And why three times, detective?"

Nia drew a deep breath and looked up, hesitating, reliving the moment. *I was pushing down cold fear and anger.*

He was a threat. I couldn't stop. "Well, he was still standing there in front of me, holding his weapon." She gestured with her hand. "It took two more shots to stop him."

The doctor stared, appearing unconvinced. "Hmm. And what were you thinking at that moment. detective?"

"Nothing." She hesitated, shaking her head. "No, that's not really true. I was scared and maybe angry. I thought I'm fucking glad he finally dropped."

"And what were you angry about, detective?"

Nia looked away glassy-eyed remembering a bloody bat dripping blood and shook her head. "Not sure."

The doctor jotted another note. "Okay. We'll leave that one for now." She looked back into her notes again. "And why were *you* the first one to arrive on scene at this B and E, detective?"

"I just happened to be in the neighborhood when the call came in that there was some sort of disturbance and the sounds of shots being fired. When I pulled up, there was a neighbor standing out front. She directed me to the third-floor apartment."

The doctor nodded. "You know that this is just part of departmental protocol any time an officer is involved in a shooting. And normally, you would be expected to wait for backup before entering an active crime scene. But given you had reason to believe there were innocent civilians in danger, your subsequent actions and use of deadly force would appear to be justified. Of course, the final determination will be up to a review board." Nia nodded, looking with furrowed brow outside the draped window at the buildings lining Melina Cass Boulevard. "But given your prior history," she paused, looking pointedly at Nia, "I need to make sure this shooting won't impact your ability to perform your duties, detective."

Nia nodded absentmindedly, not looking at the doctor. "It won't." *And there it is. I'm involved in another shooting. Now I've got 'history'.* "Are we finished, doctor?"

The doctor pushed the glasses up on her nose and looked directly at Nia. "Detective D'Amato, I'll clear you for active duty, on one condition."

How did I know there would be one condition? "And what is that doctor?"

"I'll clear you on condition you make another appointment to meet with me. After that, we can continue if you wish, or we'll be finished."

Nia made a face. "One more. I guess if that's what it takes, then one more." She stood up, shook the doctor's hand and left the room as quickly as she could.

Chapter 2

A hunched jeweler sat silently brooding, bathed in the cold glare of a cheap pole lamp. Will Caulder worked in the shadow of powerful, wealthy men, fantasizing about one day owning the precious jewels that passed through his hands every day. His body slumped in resignation as his eyes narrowed, pausing on the most recent losing lottery tickets scattered on the table. *Seems like I was born with shit luck. Horses, Dogs, Sports, Lottery. And now my bookie is pressing me to pay what I owe.* Will slowly scanned the sparsely furnished apartment. *Every night I come home to this pig sty. This is all I got to show after a dozen years of losing.* He stood and walked with a slight limp to the window, gazing with defeated eyes at the neglected gray-brown tenement buildings across the street. Looking down, he watched wind-blown litter playing chase through a gauntlet of broken bottles. He cocked his head and looked up into an overcast night sky. *That's one crazy idea, Caulder.* He shook his head, dismissing it as both fancifully absurd and beyond impossible. But once considered, however briefly, the idea persisted, consuming ever increasing amounts of his alone time.

Every night he kept returning to it again and again like an oyster lovingly caressing a tiny grain of sand. *There's no reason why I can't have some of those stones I work with every day.* He carefully considered how he might steal them and avoid being caught. *I could just take one or two stones, but they'd find out in a day or two. And then I could never go back. If I'm going to do this, it's got to be worth it. It has to be big, one of those large diamond shipments. Out of debt and more to spare.* He carefully pored over each detail that was either made part of his plan or dismissively rejected. After several weeks of compulsive planning, and stalling his increasingly impatient bookie, he knew he was nearly ready to put it into action. He sat back in his stained, upholstered chair and zealously reviewed his daring scheme like a stonecutter admiring a flawless diamond. *I think this is going to work.* He shook his head. *No. I know this is going to work.*

He tackled the easiest part of his plan first. He knew he couldn't just stuff a large number of stones in his pocket but needed a more discrete way to hide them. After searching extensively online, he found the perfect way to hide the stolen diamonds—an expandable lycra money belt. Next he purchased a hundred glass diamonds that would be more than enough to replace any shipment of diamonds. They would also buy him some additional time on Monday morning when the store manager did a cursory vault check.

He knew one of the hardest parts of his plan would be finding someone to fence the stolen gems. And diamond shipments only came in every two or three weeks, usually on Saturday, depending on business. *I need to start looking once I'm certain there'll be a shipment.*

On Tuesday morning, while sipping too hot coffee from his stained and chipped mug, he watched the shipping clerk walk by with the delivery schedule and hang it on the notice board. Will shuffled over, trying to appear disinterested while his heart pounded, blocking out all other sounds. He scanned the page and saw, near the bottom, a Saturday morning shipment of diamonds with a retail value of two million. But Will wasn't on the schedule to work! He hit the wall then looked around, hoping no one noticed. *Shit! I'm not on the schedule. I'm being pressed for the money and he's tired of my stalling. Don't want to think about what happens if I don't pay up. I can't wait any longer. Need to find a way to take the place of that idiot Tyler Gatling, this Saturday.*

On Wednesday, Will visited several pawn shops, asking about the best way to sell 'high-value merchandise, no questions asked'. He had heard that expression used on TV and thought it made him sound streetwise. None of the dealers near the Jewelers Building wanted any part of his 'merchandise.' *What good are expensive diamonds if I can't find anyone who wants them?* His face twisted in a determined scowl and he followed Washington Street south, to a rundown section of the city. He looked up at the creased and dented sign with letters missing, above a battered door. PA N HOP. Dried wine stains decorated the foundation like jagged ruby-colored spikes beneath a rusted crooked window grating. *This looks more promising.* He pushed up the collar of his coat and pushed open the battle-scarred door.

Bobby "the fence" Mastricola had a reputation for buying and selling almost anything. He had a nervous tick in his right eye that gave the impression he was always winking at you. Bobby wore a Red Sox baseball hat on backward over his slick-backed hair, and his tobacco-stained fingers were perpetually wrapped around a greasy chunk of fast food.

Will fixed what he hoped was an intimidating scowl on his face. "I have some high-end merchandise I'm looking to unload." Will spoke the word 'merchandise' slowly, lowering his voice for effect.

Bobby raised his eyebrows, cocking his head to one side. "Yeah. Good for you, pal. You a cop, or working for the cops?"

Will shot him a surprised glare, "You must be kidding. Do I *look* like a cop?"

Bobby's expression turned deadly serious. "I never kid. Answer the question or take a fuckin' hike."

Will took a deep breath. He didn't want to blow what might be his only chance. "Of course not."

"Okay. So, what kind of merchandise you got?" Will leaned closer and whispered, "High quality diamonds."

"Hmmm. How many are we talking about? " "Eighty stones with a retail value of over two million dollars."

Bobby's eyes widened momentarily in surprise. "Okay. That's a *little* outside of what I can handle. But I may know someone who *would* be interested. Give me a number where you can be reached."

Will scribbled his home number on a scrap of paper. His hand shook slightly as he wrote. "I need to hear by Thursday morning at 8:30."

Bobby nodded then looked up as he heard the pawn shop door slam open. A heavyset young man, eyes red-rimmed, hair matted, face unshaven, stood framed in the light of the doorway. He was holding a shaking gun sideways. His raspy voice echoed across the poorly-lit interior. "Nobody move!"

Will startled and started to turn towards the sound. He froze midway.

The man motioned with the barrel. "You, over there."

Will shuffled his way over to a stack of stereos and speakers lining one of the walls. The man was dressed entirely in black save for a plastic ring from a child's candy on one of his dirt-caked fingers. He inched toward the counter, gun still shaking, his eyes darting between Bobby and Will. "I want the money." Then he looked down at the display case. "And yeah. I'll take those rings too." He motioned with his head.

Bobby's face remained an impassive mask. His eyes focused like laser beams on the man in front of him. He nodded but didn't speak a word. He reached down and pulled out the tray of assorted gold and silver rings. He slowly slid off his stool, walked over to the cash register and opened it. He started

7

lifting out the cash slowly and stacking it on the counter. The man shifted his gaze from the rings to Bobby. "Come on. Come on. Hurry up!" He looked back down at the rings and started to shove handfuls into his pocket. He lowered his gun slightly. As Bobby lifted out the last of the cash, he reached with his right hand under the counter and drew out a gun from a concealed shelf. The young man looked up, sharply sucked in air, and swung his gun in Bobby's direction. There was a deafening roar. The young man was driven backward, his weapon lifted up firing aimlessly, punching a hole in the ceiling causing a rainfall of plaster chips. Bobby fired again and he dropped to the floor in a blood-stained heap.

Will stared, mouth open and ashen-faced as he inched his way toward the door. Bobby waved the gun back and forth like a teacher correcting a wayward child. "Hey, buddy, just where do you think you're going? That security camera is busted." He jerked his head to the glass eye perched over the counter. "And the cops are just looking for an excuse to bust me. So, you're my star witness. It was self-defense. Right?" He casually tilted the gun in his direction. "*And* you were just here looking to pick up a good watch cheap. Got it?" Will stared at the gun and then up at Bobby. He slowly nodded. *What the hell have I got myself into?*

Chapter 3

Detective Nia D'Amato leaned back in her cushioned swivel chair, staring out the window at two off-duty patrolmen smoking on the bottom steps of the plaza immediately in front of headquarters on Tremont Street. It reminded her of when she used to visit her Dad at the old police headquarters on Berkeley Street. She'd sneak over to the window when he left to indulge a favorite vice, smoking a stogie. The bluish smoke from the cigar would blossom from between his lips and curl up and over his balding head. Nia could almost smell the rich, sweet tobacco aroma that seemed to follow him everywhere like a fragrant apparition. When her Dad returned, he'd usually have to scold her for doing something stupid, like trying to pick up his handcuffs with a nightstick, scattering the papers on his desk everywhere. She used to wonder if she'd be smoking cigars like him when she grew up. Nia smiled at the thought.

Nia was three hours into her eight-hour shift when the phone on her desk jumped to life, jarring her out of her reverie. It came from a cruiser responding to a call about an attempted robbery and shooting at a pawn shop in a rundown section of the city on lower Washington Street. She stood up, stretched, grabbed her jacket and walked briskly through the glass-walled cubicles, her reflection flashing by at odd angles.

She remembered when her looks made her the object of precinct jokes, leering looks, and offensive remarks. Nia had more than once considered pursuing the daunting task of pressing harassment charges. But she was painfully aware of the consequences. First, she'd be ostracized by many of her fellow officers for being a snitch and not being tough enough to take the comments and ribbing that they felt was part of being a new recruit. Then she'd receive the worst duty assignments in hopes she'd resign or request a transfer out of precinct. She decided she needed to develop a thicker skin, build a repertoire of quick retorts to their bullshit, and keep working hard doing her job better than anyone else. She made a face and shook her head as she passed a middle-aged detective who raised his eyebrow and stared at her as she passed. "In your dreams, Butler." *Well, I've earned the respect of some of them, but there's still too many knuckle draggers in this place.* Seven years ago, she had passed her detective grade exam and been awarded her new badge. Six months later a position opened, and she put in long grueling hours determined to show that she was more than capable in her new role. She learned there was a price to pay for her dedication and hard work.

She got into her cruiser, turned on the flashing lights and felt the familiar rush of adrenaline as the car sped out of the precinct lot. A cluster of runners streamed by in a colorful blur of nylon running pants and warm-up jackets. *The last time I jogged with a group was at police academy training in Hyde Park. Every morning at 7:30 we'd all leave the facility on Washington Street and jog a half-dozen miles, winding through parts of Milton and Readville, before returning to that closed elementary school. There were always a few stragglers returning a few minutes later to a torrent of harassment throughout the day by the instructors. Everyone had to complete that killer six-mile course in under forty-eight minutes to pass one of the physical requirements. I was determined never to find myself in that group of stragglers.*

There were two cruisers with lights flashing outside the pawnshop when Nia arrived. She ducked under the tape and walked up to the officer who secured the crime scene. He looked up and nodded. "Detective. We have one adult male, age early twenties, dead from two bullets fired by the owner, Bobby Mastricola. Apparently, the deceased had come into the pawnshop holding a gun and demanding money. The owner had started to comply and then he pulled out a gun hidden under the counter. There was an exchange of gunfire and our perp," he motioned with his head toward the open pawnshop door, "got the worst of it. The M.E. is on his way."

Nia nodded. "Were there any witnesses to the incident?"

He looked through his notes as he spoke. "Yes. There was one witness, William Caulder. He was inside checking out the merchandise when the perp entered. He's over there, leaning against the cruiser. And I'm sure you already know Bobby Mastricola."

Nia made a face and shook her head. "Unfortunately." She donned booties and latex gloves before entering the pawn shop. She stood over the body, considering the dead man sprawled on the floor. He had taken two bullets to the chest, eyes still open in surprise. He hadn't shaven in several days and his were clothes dirty and torn in places. Nia bent down. *You look like you've been living on the mean streets for a while, buddy.* She turned his arm over and saw needle tracks. *And you picked the wrong place to rob for drug money.* Nia looked around and walked over to a pair of old stereo speakers. She bent down and picked up a weapon by the trigger guard, inspecting it. *One spent round and no other bullets in the chamber.* She replaced the weapon, then stood up and surveyed the interior of the pawnshop. There were bits of plaster littering the floor. She looked up. *I think I know where we'll find your bullet.* The dingy tobacco-stained ceiling now sported a round hole ringed with a starkly white crater of plaster missing around the edges. It was several feet away from where the robber collapsed. The counter at the far end of the shop stood like an oasis of calm surrounded on two sides by a chaotic jumble of cast-off items traded for their thirty pieces of silver. Nia left the shop to question Will Caulder. He was still leaning

11

against the squad car, looking nervously around, anxious to leave.

He looked at her, a fearful expression etched on his pale complexion. "Will Caulder? I want to ask you a few questions." He gave a small nod. "I see your address is on Sever Street in Roxbury." Another small nod. What brought you to the pawn shop today, Mr. Caulder?"

He looked quickly down, appearing to search for answers on the graffiti scrawled sidewalk . "Ah, I hoped to find a deal on a really good watch."

Nia nodded slowly, not really convinced by his answer. "What kind of watch were you looking for Mr. Caulder?" *His eyes are searching for an answer. He's not very good at this.*

"Ah, I kind of like Seiko watches. They make some really good ones." He looked away not meeting her gaze.

"And what kind of work do you do, Mr. Caulder?"

"I'm a bench jeweler at E.B. Horn in downtown crossing."

"Yes, I know the place." She looked around for a parked vehicle. And you came from work?" A nod. "So how did you get here?"

"I walked."

"I see. You are a *long* way from work." Another brief nod. Nia gave him a questioning look. "Okay. Now what can you tell me about what happened here, starting when the man who was shot walked in?"

"Not a lot to tell. It all happened so fast." He put his hands up and went silent.

Nia leaned toward him. "Please continue Mr. Caulder."

Will looked up. "Oh, yeah. Well, this guy walks in waving a gun and yells at the man working behind the counter to give him all of his cash. Then he sees all of the rings inside the case and tells him he wants them too. So, while he's looking down and grabbing the rings, the guy behind the counter pulls out a gun and shoots him. He sort of staggers backward and his gun goes off, once I think. Then, the guy shoots him again."

"And what were you doing all this time, Mr. Caulder?"

"Oh, well when he came in, he told me to move over to the side by a bunch of speakers. That's where I was when he got shot."

"Then what did you do?"

"My first thought was to get the hell out of there. I didn't want anything to do with a shooting. So, I started to leave, and the guy behind the counter waved his gun and told me to stay cause I was his witness to what happened."

"Anything else?"

"Nope. I've just been waiting here for you guys to question me."

Nia pointed at his wrist. "I see you own a pretty fine watch already. It looks like one of those fancy Citizen brand watches. A look of fear creased his face and his eyes twitched from side to side like.

"Well, yeah." He hesitated, thinking. "You see, I've been having problems with this one and thought I might find another expensive watch here for less money."

She gave him a skeptical look. "You know, there are lots of pawnshops closer to where you work, Mr. Caulder."

He opened his mouth then closed it. "Well, I searched for some pawnshops online that looked like I could get a good deal. I guess I didn't realize how far away this one was."

Nia closed her notebook, still unconvinced. "I see. Thank you, Mr. Caulder." She turned to go, then stopped and turned back to Caulder who had already started to leave. "Oh, one more thing. Did you find a Seiko you liked?"

He looked at her puzzled. "What?"

Nia looked back through her notes. "You said you were looking for a Seiko watch."

"Oh that. Ah, yeah, I did see one. But we were interrupted when that guy came in waving a gun."

"Okay, Mr. Caulder." She pointed her pen at him. "That should do it for now. We have your contact information in case we need to follow up with you again." Will stood looking worried for a moment, then turned and walked back up Washington Street as fast as his uneven gait would permit. Nia watched his receding figure, a troubled expression on her face. *What were you really doing in this pawnshop, Mr. Caulder?*

Bobby 'The Fence' Mastricola was slouched near a corner of the brick pawnshop façade, a barely visible cigarette dangling from between his lips and yellowish-brown stained teeth. Nia knew Bobby well. He was never too far away from whatever shady dealing was taking place on lower Washington Street. He rolled his eyes as he saw her approach and held up his hands. "Detective, this was self-defense. You saw the guy on the floor, *and* I got a witness who'll swear to it."

"Bobby." She shook her head. "Why is it that you are always around whenever something bad happens?"

He shrugged. His face broke into a thin smile that never reached his eyes. "Bad luck detective. It's all just bad luck."

Nia smirked. "Right, all just bad luck. Okay. You've done this before. Tell me what happened and start with Mr. Caulder coming into the shop." Nia listened to him recount the sequence of events around the attempted robbery. *His story matches Will Caulder's almost word for word. Almost.*

"So tell me Bobby about this watch Mr. Caulder was looking to buy."

Bobby stretched back and looked up. Well, he was looking to pick up a good watch, probably for small money. But we were interrupted and never got that far."

"And what kind of a watch was he interested in?"

Bobby shrugged. "Don't know. Like I said, we didn't get that far cause we were interrupted."

Nia nodded. "Okay. I think we're done for now, Bobby."

So one of them, maybe both, are lying. Caulder was here for another reason. They didn't need much time before the cruiser arrived to make up a cover story, but why? A bench jeweler, looking to buy an expensive watch in this dump doesn't make any sense. She shook her head in frustration. Nia stayed at the pawnshop until the crime scene photographer finished taking pictures and the medical examiner took the body away. She stood outside, reflecting on the dingy exterior before heading back to the station. *A bench jeweler and a pawnshop owner meet here to discuss, something. They're interrupted by a junkie.* Nia made a face. *I know there's more to this story.*

Chapter 4

Will spent a sleepless night tossing, turning and jumping at every muffled sound coming from other tenants in the thin-walled, tired old building. He couldn't stop seeing the bloody body of the junkie lying twisted on the floor. *Fuck. I haven't stolen anything and there's already one dead guy. Was this shooting a sign of more bad things to come? And how long will it take the cops to put two and two together?* He knew if they connected the robbery at E.B. Horn back to him and then the pawnshop, they might be able to track him down. *No,. I'll be long gone.* He shook his head still trying to lose two haunting dead eyes.

The first rays of early morning light sliced through the frayed edges of the pale-yellow shade. *Why is it when I just start to get comfortable it's always time to get up?* Will reluctantly swung his legs over the side of the mattress and sat, shaking his head, still pursued by dark images and plagued by lingering doubts. *Maybe it wouldn't be such a bad thing if Bobby's contact doesn't call.* He heaved a deep sigh. *No. This is a good plan. A little bad luck doesn't mean it won't work.* He gritted his teeth. *I can't quit. I'm so close. I can almost smell all those stacks of green.* Despite his resolve to continue, he worried his plan would hit a more serious, unforeseen hurdle and shatter like a bottle of cheap wine. He was just finishing a bowl of mushy cereal, when the phone rang causing him to jump, splashing milk and soggy flakes cross the table. He waited until it rang three times. *Don't want to appear too eager to make this deal.* He lowered his voice an octave and answered, "Hello."

The voice on the other end replied, "Bobby tells me you may have some merchandise to sell."

"Maybe. If the price is right."

"And exactly what are you selling?"

"High-end diamonds."

"How many are we talking about?"

"Eighty."

"High-end? Exactly what kind of quality?"

This was one area that Will felt supremely confident. He knew a diamond's color evaluation was based on the absence of color. A chemically pure and structurally perfect diamond has no hue, not unlike a drop of distilled water, and consequently, it has a higher value and would be rated D, E, or F. A color grading of G through J would be near colorless and have a higher value than those rated K (faint color) through Z (more color). The high clarity rating of VVS1 meant there'd be very, very slight inclusions that would be extremely difficult for a professional to see under ten times magnification.

"These are top of the line, highest quality diamonds. Color grade for all of them is F. Clarity is VVS1 or higher, and they range in size from one to two and a half carats. That's two million in high-end round cut diamonds." He hesitated, momentarily second-guessing the amount he had planned to ask for. "And you can steal then for one million."

Benny, no stranger to diamonds, smiled. He knew if what this guy was saying was true, he could be looking at making some serious money for a change.

"You must be new to this business, pal. That's not even close. We can't sell the diamonds for two million. Maybe half, and that's if we're lucky. We are willing to pay…" There was a lengthy pause. Will held his breath, rubbing his thumb and index finger together in anticipation, waiting for the big number. "Ten cents on the dollar, that's one hundred thousand dollars. And that's *if* they're as high quality as you say."

Will's face flushed crimson. *No fucking way. This guy's trying to rip me off.* He shouted into the phone, his voice rising in anger. "What! They *are* high quality! "Go to hell." He slammed the receiver down, surprised at the vehemence of his reaction. He stared at the phone, breathing heavy. *I know. I should have made a counteroffer, but ten cents on the dollar. What a fucking insult. Now what do I do? I've just blown off my only lead to sell the diamonds Smart move.* The phone rang again. He answered "Hello" with far less assurance than the first time.

"Nobody hangs up on me. Do it again and I will find you. My offer is one hundred thousand. Take it, if you want to stay healthy."

Just what I need. Another goon trying to hurt me. Will knew it was far less than the real value of the diamonds, but he knew he had limited options and was also feeling the pressure of unspoken violence from his bookie. "You got yourself a deal. Hey, what's your name?"

"Benny. Do you have the stones with you?"

"Not yet. I'll have them Saturday."

"Okay. We'll meet at Public Alley 438 behind Arlington Street Church around 12:15 on Saturday. I will inspect the stones, and if they're as good as you claim, we'll make the switch."

"What? Meet you in an alley? No fucking way. I'm not that crazy. We need to meet in a *very* public place."

"Public place. Okay. Let's see. How about around noon outside the Black Seed Cafe and Grille on Tremont Street? We'll go inside, grab a table, and make the switch. Is that public enough for you?"

"Yeah. That'll work. And I think I know that place. It's not far from where I work. How will I know you?"

"Don't worry about that Caulder. Just wait out front, and I'll find you."

There was a click; Benny hung up. Will sat staring at the phone, startled to hear Benny say his name. He sat for a moment, puzzling over how Benny would know. *Benny and Bobby probably do a lot of business together. I'll bet they exchange a lot more than just names and telephones numbers.* Will glanced up at the clock startled to see he only had just enough time to make it into work.

Will had trouble focusing on his work all morning. He hadn't yet come up with a plan of how he was going to incapacitate Tyler on Friday so that he'd be unable to go to work the next day. He looked over at Tyler working at the next bench. Sticking out of his back pocket he could just make out the words 'Justice League' on the cover of a comic book. He smiled as he saw another piece of the puzzle come together.

After work, Will walked to a nearby CVS drugstore and bought a bottle of ipecac syrup. He remembered once when his mother thought he had eaten some poisonous berries and she forced him to drink ipecac syrup mixed with ginger ale. It didn't take too long before he spent the rest of the day throwing up the berries and much, much more. As he walked down the aisle to the register, he stopped, looking at a bottle with a familiar label. *MiraLAX. Nasty stuff!* Will remembered drinking it with Gatorade as part of his colonoscopy preparation. He decided he would leave nothing here to chance. He picked up the bottle and continued to the checkout line, smiling in anticipation.

Chapter 5

Benjamin Penny was a small-time hood courting big-time dreams. He grew up in a tough neighborhood ready to fight anyone who teased him with the nickname: bad Penny. He quickly learned to be smart about who to fight, who to ally with, and who to later seek revenge on. Benny's life in crime started when he was in fourth grade with acts of vandalism against anyone giving him grief, shoplifting pocket-sized things he wanted, and occasionally stealing from anyone weak, old or defenseless. Before he started to shave his sparse facial hairs in junior high, he joined a street gang and quickly graduated to robbery, assault, and carjacking. Benny earned a reputation for being a sly, devious punk who knew how to get a job done and slip away quietly without being noticed.

His ability to sense trouble helped him avoid being picked up by the police when they would make one of their periodic 'gang sweeps' designed to reassure a crime-weary public. After one particularly successful gang sweep, he decided it was time to start working independently, doing mostly breaking and entering and burglaries, particularly jewelry stores. He was smart enough not to hit too many stores in one area, and he spaced his robberies out over time, so the police didn't suspect a pattern. But the jewelry store heists and subsequent sale of items on the black market did catch the attention of one man: Luciano 'Lou' Vitelli. He was the crime boss who ran much of the gambling, drugs, and prostitution in parts of downtown Boston and the South End. He also kept a close eye on what merchandise was being traded on the black market and noticed a steady trickle of jewelry from recent heists around the city. He became most interested in this activity.

Benny was familiar with the name Lou Vitelli. He had heard stories about him, cruel and ruthless, and never wanted to meet him. Years earlier, he had briefly considered working directly with some of the pawnshops in the area until he heard about the bullet-riddled body of another small-time crook who had apparently also thought it was too good an idea to pass up.

He lived in a run-down high rise under an assumed name and had just left the apartment to case his next heist. He never saw the two men waiting for him just out of sight as he left the building. They both suddenly appeared and blocked his way. "Mr. Penny. Mr. Vitelli would like to talk to you."

How the fuck did I miss these two slabs of beef? "Sorry. You have the wrong guy, pal." He turned to walk away.

A heavy hand fell on his shoulder. "Don't be stupid, Penny."

Shit. Two fucking goons. He nodded fearing this would be a one-way ride. They escorted him to a black caddy waiting solemnly by the curb. *Looks like a hearse, how fucking appropriate.*

Lou Vitelli worked in the North End in the back of a storefront on Salem Street that sold Italian pastries. Benny stood in front of the smiling crime boss feeling like an insect on a mounting board. "Mr. Benjamin Penny. Please, have a seat." He gestured to one of two chairs. "I've been hearing a lot about you lately. May I call you Benny?"

You can call me Ismael as long as you don't fucking whack me. Benny nodded grim faced, nervously rubbing the leather pull on the zipper of his jacket.

"Well, Benny. It has come to my attention that some of your recent activity has taken place in my jurisdiction. And I'm *sure* it was unintentional." He leaned menacingly toward Benny placing both hands on his desk. "It *was* unintentional. Right, Benny?"

"Ah. Yes Mr. Vitelli. I don't know exactly where your jurisdiction is."

"Well Benny, that's not going to be a problem anymore." There was a long pause as Vitelli stared hard at the suddenly hunched figure.

Benny clenched his teeth swallowing hard. *Ah, shit. Here it comes.* He looked down and winced, waiting. *The last fucking thing I'll ever see, is my god damn scuffed shoes.*

Vitelli cleared his throat. "I want you to work for me."

Benny looked up at the imposing figure, hesitating. Relief flooded through him. "Ah. Can I think it over, Mr. Vitelli?"

Vitelli smiled a cruel smile. "You've either got brass balls or you're really even more stupid than you look. This *is* your chance Benny, and it's your *only* chance."

Benny appeared to shrink. *Fuck. It's his way or the highway...a one-way ticket to the morgue.* "Okay. I'm working for you now Mr. Vitelli."

***

And that was the first day I worked with pawnshops run by Vitelli, fencing items that were too expensive or too hot for them to handle. Of course, Vitelli always takes a generous share. Whenever I need a lot of cash to complete a deal, I visit Vitelli. He lets me 'borrow' what I need for a few days. I have to pay it back at crazy rates. That's the price of doing business in Vitelli's territory with his blessing and I have the benefit of his protection from any interference. And Vitelli does allow me to supplement my income with jewelry store heists, but he always gets a healthy piece of the action.

Benny arrived at the North End bakery...an innocuous front for the crime boss's operation. He needed to see Vitelli about a large diamond purchase that seemed too good to pass up. He always looked forward to the mouth-watering aroma of freshly baked bread, but never his conversations with the boss. A tiny bell announced his arrival. There were mostly matronly Italian women working behind the counter except at the cash register. A short, balding, heavyset man with scarring around his eyes looked up as Benny entered. He recognized the former heavyweight boxer as he walked up to the register. "I need to see Vitelli about some pawnshop business." The man pressed a button under the counter and motioned with his head to a door behind him.

The door opened into a small waiting room guarded by two powerfully built men who looked like they could be bodybuilders. The older one was completely bald, and his white collared shirt showed dark sweat stains under both arms. The other man was younger, wore a David Ortiz Red Sox t-shirt and had longish dark brown hair which was tied up in a man bun. They were sitting at a small table, both were sporting shoulder holsters with guns. The younger man stood and walked over to Benny as he entered the room. "You know the drill."

He sighed, turned around, and placed his hands on the wall. "Bull, you know I don't carry."

Bull nodded but said nothing. He patted him down looking for concealed weapons or a wire. He looked up and announced to a tiny camera above an ornate mirror on the wall, "He's clean." A concealed door on the other side of the room clicked open. Both men stood aside. "Mr. Vitelli will see you now."

Benny entered the finely appointed office and approached the desk. The two bodyguards followed him in and stood on either side of the door. He had only gone to see Vitelli a handful of times before. But the amount he was asking for this time was much more than any of the previous amounts. He knew his cut always seemed to wind up less when he was forced to borrow money from Vitelli. *But these diamonds should be worth plenty. With a deal this big, I should be able to negotiate a bigger cut. Vitelli will still make a bundle.*

Lou Vitelli was always impeccably dressed like he worked in a corner office of a high-rise corporate building conducting senior-level management meetings. Today Vitelli was wearing an expensive looking gray three-piece suit with a matching tie and narrow pin-striped shirt. His face was deeply tanned and sported a neatly trimmed beard. His eyes were deep brown, and he always wore his hair close-cropped. He sat behind an intricately carved mahogany desk that had a small stack of papers neatly stacked on one side and a computer monitor and keyboard on the other. "Benny, have a seat." Benny dropped into one of two chairs facing the desk. "I understand you need my help acquiring some valuable merchandise."

Benny ran a tongue across his upper lip and took a breath. "Yes. Mr. Vitelli. I am looking to buy eighty high-quality diamonds from a jewelry company employee who works for…"

Vitelli held up his hands and briefly turned his head to one side. "Benny. I don't want to know where this merchandise comes from. How much did you say that *we* are willing to pay for these diamonds?"

It wasn't lost on Benny that Vitelli had just used the words 'that *we* are willing to pay for the diamonds.' "I made an offer of $100,000 and it was accepted, after some initial resistance."

Vitelli's eyes momentarily expressed surprise. "*That* is a lot of money, Benny. Do you have confidence in the value of these diamonds?"

Benny rushed to explain. "Yes, sir I do. I'd estimate the retail value to be about two million."

Vitelli nodded slowly. "So, we might see a black-market value of about one million. If what you say is true, that would make this transaction quite lucrative. So, if we move forward with this purchase, we will need to settle a few small details." He put his fingertips together in front of him. "Like my share of the diamonds."

Benny frowned. *I don't like the way this is going. Vitelli is looking at a bigger piece of the pie than I figured. Fuck it. I can't lose my nerve now.* "Well sir, since I'm assuming most of the risk in this business transaction, I thought it would be fair if we would split the diamonds fifty-fifty."

Vitelli smiled at Benny displaying two rows of perfect, white teeth. He slowly shook his head. "Oh, Benny Penny. What can you be thinking? I'm afraid that's not what *I* had in mind at all."

Motherfucker looks like a god damn shark. "Mr. Vitelli, I'm doing all the work here and you're looking to make a shitload of money on this deal."

Vitelli paused and looked over at Benny, nodding patiently, like a father needing to explain something to his slow son. "This is true, Benny. But perhaps you have forgotten that *I* would be supplying all the money for this transaction. And without that money," he turned his hands up in front of him and stared down at Benny, "there would be no deal."

Benny waited while Vitelli pondered his share, looking up at the ceiling. *Oh crap. How big a cut is he thinking?* He followed Vitelli's gaze and realized he was staring at several bullet holes scaring the smooth plaster.

A soft, cool voice brought his attention back to the smiling crime boss. "I was thinking more ninety-five percent for me and five percent for you."

Benny jumped up, and the chair fell over. "What? That's crazy. I'm bringing the deal to you. I'm doing all the dirty work and taking all the risk. You got to at least give me more than a measly five percent."

When the chair fell, the two guards rested their hands on the guns in their shoulder holster and started to move forward. Vitelli looked at them and gave his head a slight shake. The guards stopped, hands still poised on the gun handles. Benny's voice trailed off to silence as he remembered where he was and who he was talking to. Bull moved forward, picked up the chair and pushed it against Benny's legs. Benny sat down slowly, his eyes fixed on Lou.

Vitelli shook his head. His tone of voice changed to the hard-nosed head of a highly profitable underworld operation. He leaned back in his chair and tapped the ends of his fingers together. "Benny. I *don't* think you understand. We are not doing some negotiation here. I am making *you* a generous offer. After we subtract the money we pay, I will be letting you walk away with about $45,000 in diamonds, minus just a couple of thousand in interest on the money you are borrowing." He leaned forward on his desk and stared down at him, a small smile playing on his lips. "Now I don't consider that bad pay for just a couple of hours work. Wouldn't you agree, Benny?"

Dead silence. Benny glared, not responding immediately. *If looks could kill, you'd be splattered all over the paneled fucking wall in back of you.* The tense silence was broken only by the faint hum of some distant machine. His reply was barely audible through clenched teeth, "Yes, Mr. Vitelli."

Vitelli leaned back in his chair. "Good, good. I *knew* you'd understand. Now tell me, when will this purchase take place?"

"We're meeting at noon on Saturday over lunch."

"So, I should expect to see you on Saturday. Let's say by 1:30?

"Well, I guess I should be able to make it here by then." Vitelli stood up, putting his hands on the desk. "Then I think we are set. Just follow Rocco when you leave. He'll see you get the $100,000."

After Benny left, Vitelli turned to Bull. "Follow our slippery friend. And don't let him out of your sight. If you need an extra pair of eyes, take Rocco along too."

***

Benny's face was set in an angry scowl. *That really burns my ass. Five percent!* Benny knew he'd be making decent money, but far less than his usual twenty percent. *No choice! If I walk away, I get nothing. And once I asked for the money, I can't go anywhere else without getting wacked.*

Benny looked back over his shoulder. *Feels like I'm being followed. Probably one of his goons. Never done that before.* He frowned. *At least, I don't think he has. Doesn't trust me with that much money.* He smiled. *Maybe he shouldn't.* Benny reached the doors to his Harrison Court apartment building in the South End. He quickly looked behind him, hoping to catch one of Lou's guards watching him. *Nothing suspicious. Wait!* Benny spotted someone leaning against a storefront across the street looking his way. *One of his bodyguards?* He was puzzled at first, that the bodyguard didn't try to hide. *Of course. They want me to know so I don't try anything.*

Benny let himself into the lobby and then took the elevator to his modest studio apartment on the third floor. He locked and bolted the door, then carried the case over to a small desk under the bay window overlooking a tree-lined brick patio. Looking up, he made a face, seeing the bodyguard still slouched against the building across the street. He walked over to the liquor cabinet, took out a bottle of bourbon with a stylized black label. Pulling out the cork, he poured himself two fingers, held it up to the light, then swirled the caramel-colored liquid around and took a sip. *Bastards will probably have someone watching till I'm back at Vitelli's with the diamonds.* He sauntered back to the small table, setting down the drink. He slid the catches back on the briefcase, slowly opening the cover. He stood gazing at the stacks of green carpeting the inside. He picked up his drink and took another sip. *I'd have to be crazy. The last guy who tried going into business for himself ended up on a slab. But that was different. He was muscling in on Vitelli's territory.* He looked back at the piles of green. *Yeah, this would be so much worse.*

Benny couldn't tear his eyes away from the briefcase. A gnawing desire burned deep. He knew all the big jobs that should have earned him some serious money had left him with little to show for it. He thought this would be the job, that once in a lifetime job. But Vitelli would be the one to walk away with close to a million dollars in diamonds. *What will I walk away with? Yeah, more fucking small change.* Benny had planned to salt away enough to retire someplace warm before somebody retired him, permanently. That always seemed to get pushed off to some big score in the future. *Yeah, good luck with Vitelli and that retirement plan.* Benny closed the briefcase lid and looked down at his empty glass. *I definitely need more of this tonight.* He walked back to the liquor cabinet, took out the bottle of bourbon, pulled the cork, and poured himself a healthy splash. He held it up and tilted the glass, looking broodingly at the golden-brown liquid. *And there's no better companion to help me think. Could this be my big score, my chance to finally retire?* He looked down into his drink, his features shifting and morphing on its rolling surface as he flirted with dangerous ideas. He slowly lifted his glass high in a toast to something unseen, then drained it.

Chapter 6

Nia sat with her feet perched on the edge of the gray slate coffee table. She watched the never-ending series of headlights slowly snake their way north out of the city after crossing the white-cabled Zakim bridge. She looked down at the nearly empty glass of tequila lightly resting on her stomach. Nia tried to limit herself to no more than one drink, but lately found that increasingly difficult. She lifted the glass; ice cubes clinked, sliding to hit her lip. She closed her eyes, slowly drawing in air through pursed lips. *Oh that's helps.* But Nia knew there was no relief from the seemingly endless string of shootings, stabbings, and violence that oozed from every dank, dark recess of the city like a festering wound. As the ice melted into the remaining traces of agave nectar, she drifted off unbidden, to a long-ago time and too familiar place.

***

I leave my mom watching TV, knowing she'd fall asleep, slouched over a ball of yarn and knitting needles, working on some unlucky relative's Christmas sweater. I trudge upstairs, following my nightly routine of going to my room to study for a few hours, watch a little TV, and then slip off to sleep before midnight. But tonight, something feels different. I lower my Chemistry book and listen intently, watching moonlight shadowed tree branches dance with wild abandon across my tattered window shades. Our house is old and has always made odd, creepy noises, especially at night. I remember my Dad laughing when I would creep terrified into my parent's bedroom at night. He'd explain in a quivering, supposed-to-be-scary voice that it might be our old furnace and hot water pipes shuddering and shaking the night away or it could be just the wind-tossed branches scratching at the windows trying to get in. Then he'd pull back the covers to make room for me to sleep safely between him and a disapproving Mom. But now I'm seventeen and used to all the odd noises, and Dad's been dead for a couple of years. So there's just Mom and me to ward off the not so scary monsters left from my childhood.

Another noise. It's louder now and mixed in with harsh voices. I drop my book and look up, frowning at the door. Are my childhood monsters real? They don't sound like they're very far outside my room. I slip off the bed, my heart pounding like a caged animal trying to break free. I look around for something to chase whatever it is, away. My favorite baseball bat! I pick it up, my hands slippery with sweat. I wipe them on my pajama pants. I slowly open my bedroom door. The voices are clearer now. I frown. It's men's voices. What are men doing in my house? My mother is screaming for them to get out. Sudden silence. Now she's crying for them to stop - to stop what? Oh shit. No, not that. I grit my teeth. That's not going to happen. Every breath hurts as I lurch forward, stumbling on the hallway rug. I reach out my free hand for the wall to steady myself. I stop, paralyzed with fear at the top of the stairs. Another piercing terrified scream echoes through the house stabbing my heart. A dull heat surges through me, every nerve burning white hot. I am consumed; my world floods blood red. I walk past a partly open door into my parent's darkened bedroom.

Men on the floor. My mother's body thrashing between them, her face angry, terrified, her arms pinned by a man in a gray hoodie. He smiles at her terror. Another man straddles her legs, fumbling with his pants. They stare intently, devouring her with hungry wolf eyes. I grip the bat with both hands and lift off the ground, screaming in primal rage, bringing it down on the first man's head. He issues a short-surprised shriek;

blood spatters. He rolls off my mother onto the floor. The second man looks up open-mouthed, momentarily startled, then scrambles to his feet. I swing the bat sideways catching him on the side of his head sending him crashing against the rocking chair. He holds his head, getting to his knees, bellowing an incoherent stream of profanities. I walk over, lift the bloody club, and drive it down again, sending him sprawling, face cracking against the hardwood floor. Both men lay unmoving, slowly oozing red-stained pools. I turn and look back at my mother. She is sitting, her arms holding her legs, rocking and quietly weeping. My bat clatters to the floor. I fall beside her, my body racked with uncontrollable sobs.

***

Nia awoke with a start, her hand slapping the glass sending it skidding, tumbling over on the coffee table. She watched the melted cubes spread and darken the slate like so many creeping liquid fingers. She threw a napkin to hide her clumsiness, then stretched and wandered over to the window, gazing across a city alive with lights in the distance. *I lost Dad, couldn't let that happen to Mom.* She took a deep breath, gazing across time at the bodies of two men on the floor of their old house. Nia stopped and chewed on the inside of her cheek, considering her troubled reflection in the glass, scarred and broken by moving lights in the distance. *I hate that feeling, like there's someone else, someone scary in charge. Is that why I became a cop?* The distant muffled drone of highway traffic was the only reply.

Chapter 7

Tyler Gatling, a bench jeweler who had worked at E.B. Horn for three years, had no ambition to move up in the business, or really in any particular direction. He lived at home, was partial to junk food, superheroes and anything to do with anime. On Friday morning, he walked into work, thinking about sneaking extra break time to read his latest issue of the Justice League and what he wanted for lunch...a double bacon cheeseburger with extra french fries. Will intercepted him as he slumped into his chair at the next workbench.

"Tyler, I've been reading some interesting facts about the founding members of the Justice League online." Tyler turned to face him looking mildly surprised. Will had never shown any interest in superheroes in the past. Will started to recite what he had learned. "This fan website said there are six official members of the Justice League." Will stopped, pursing his lips, thinking hard about the six names. "Let's see, there's Superman, Batman, Wonder Woman, Flash, Aquaman, and Green Lantern."

Tyler responded in disbelief. "What? Are you on drugs, Caulder? There are SEVEN founding members. You left out Martian Manhunter!"

Will slowly shook his head. "No. I'm sure I have that right. I read it online just last night." He turned pointing at Tyler, his face a mask of certainty. "I'll tell you what, if I'm wrong, I'll buy you lunch today."

A hungry grin slowly spread across Tyler's face. "Deal." He pulled the Justice League comic book out of his back pocket. He pointed to each of the seven characters on the cover, reciting their names. He tossed it over on Will's table. "Read it and weep, Caulder." He pushed out his stomach and patted it. "You owe me lunch, and I'm feeling really hungry today."

Will took a moment to respond, his mouth open, looking carefully at each character on the cover then back up at Tyler. He did his best to react with a look of shock and disbelief. "Well, I'll be dammed! I can't believe that stupid website was wrong. I'm going to let them know how badly they screwed up." He grudgingly looked up. "Well, a bet's a bet. It looks like I'll be buying you lunch today, Tyler."

At lunchtime, Will bought Tyler's favorite lunch and then drizzled unflavored ipecac syrup over the artery-clogging bacon double cheeseburger. Next, he opened up the super-sized container of cherry Coke and stirred in Miralax. Tyler was waiting for him when he returned, greedily taking his lunch and heading to the small staff room. Will watched with quiet amusement as Tyler wolfed down the doctored sandwich and cherry Coke exclaiming "Boy, you weren't kidding! I guess you *were* starving!"

Tyler replied through food stuffed cheeks "I was really famished. This is my favorite lunch. And it tastes even *better* when someone else buys it for me." He chuckled, causing bits of food and soda to spray onto the table.

Will looked at him, smiling broadly. "I'm glad you like it." *And Tyler, you'll never know how good it really tastes until you get to sample it again when it's on the way up and out.*

They had just started back to work on the bench about thirty minutes after lunch, when Tyler looked over at Will and began to complain. "Hey, my freaking stomach. It feels kind of funny." He rubbed his belly and started to moan.

Will stared open-mouthed in mock concern. "Maybe you ate that sandwich too fast. Why don't you rest your head on the bench for a few minutes?" Tyler took his advice, continuing to groan softly. Will took the opportunity to alert their boss that Tyler was not feeling well. Mr. Resnick followed Will back down to the work area to check on Tyler. He approached the moaning, hunched figure, putting his hand on Tyler's shoulder. "Tyler, I'm sorry you don't feel well. Maybe you should take the rest of the day off." Tyler suddenly sat up and turned, his face chalky white, his stomach shaking and rumbling like a dormant volcano ready to erupt. Without warning an eruption of vomit exploded out his mouth, a liquid projectile, splattering against the front of his horrified boss.

Mr. Resnick looked down in disgust, at the chunky liquid layer coating his shirt, pants, and shoes. He backed away exclaiming, "Shit, shit, SHIT!" Tyler raced for the bathroom on the other side of the room, mumbling a litany of "Sorry, sorry, so sorry." Resnick stared at his ruined suit as he sputtered, "Damn it! This was my *favorite* suit!" He then looked up, suddenly remembering that Tyler was scheduled to work Saturday morning. "This is just great. If he's *this* sick there's *no* way he can work tomorrow!"

Will raised a hand to get his boss's attention. "Wait sir. If Tyler is unable to work tomorrow, I'd be happy to come in and take his place."

Resnick turned. "Why, thank you, Mr. Caulder. The company appreciates your willingness to step in and help out."

"Sir, I'm only too happy to help him out," he replied with feigned concern for his sick colleague.

At the end of an eventful day, Will dragged himself home and threw himself into the lumpy overstuffed chair. His head ached from lack of sleep and the stressful events of the day. He managed a small smile as he recalled a miserable Tyler Gatling, throwing up all over his boss, and then running into the bathroom, spending the rest of the day anchored to the toilet with unrelenting diarrhea.

That part of my plan worked perfectly. His face turned serious. *I'm still worried about tomorrow.* He knew any one of the things he had to do, could go terribly wrong.

Chapter 8

Will awoke with a start, still sitting from the night before in the stuffed chair that faced the window. His eyes were wide and unfocused, his shirt stained with a cold sweat. It was a nightmare that never changed since he began plotting his escape from an intolerable existence. He was running, endlessly running. Pockets crammed full of diamonds pressed sharp and hard against his skin, stabbing him with every tortured step. He desperately tried to escape from some unimaginable terror, but despite running as hard as he could, every step was in agonizingly slow motion. From behind him came the relentless pounding echo of footsteps getting louder and louder, closer and still closer. His heart pounded ferociously. Sweat trickled down his forehead and into his eyes, stinging and blinding him. Then without warning he would slip on something soft and decaying underfoot. He'd lose his balance, pitch forward onto a bed of jagged broken bottles and roll in agony onto his back, gasping for air in the terrifying blackness. A blinding flash of pain would stab his stomach. And then he'd wake up, dripping wet.

Will stripped off his damp clothes and shuffled quickly through the chilly air to the bathroom. He pushed aside the mildewed curtain around the ancient claw-footed tub, adjusted the water and stepped over the high enameled side. He muttered short grunts of approval as he reviewed each part of his plan, absentmindedly pushing the soap across his nearly hairless chest. Will dried and dressed hurriedly in black jeans, a blue collared shirt, and a lined Patriot's jacket. In his haste, he almost forgot to put on the money belt that already held the fake glass replacement diamonds in four inside pockets. He double-checked everything he'd need and stuffed his few remaining valuables into an oversized lunch bag. He walked to the door, pausing with his hand on the knob. *I'm leaving this dump for the last time.* He turned, casting his eyes around the shabby interior littered with second-hand furniture. *Twelve years. And this crap is all I have to show for it.* He closed the door to the apartment and stopped. *This is it. No turning back now.* He walked down the stairs, bouncing slightly. *They won't make fun of me when I have money.*

He walked through his neighborhood with furrowed brow and a steely focus. His eyes looked to his new life in a new country far beyond the pathetic row after row of neglected brownstones, shifting piles of blackened litter and sweet, rancid odor of decaying garbage. *This'll all soon be bad memories, if everything goes well. And it has to, it just has to.* He continued past the fancy front entrance of E.B. Horn, turned the corner and walked up a short flight of grated metal steps to the employee entrance. Phil, the short powerfully-built black guard at the door, greeted him with a friendly, "Morning Mr. Caulder!"

"Uh, hi Phil."

"My bones are telling me there's bad weather on the way."

A warning bell sounded in the back of Will's mind. *Snow is not part of my plan. If it starts too early, I might have to find another way to leave the city.* "Well I hope it can hold off until I finish at noon today, Phil. I didn't come prepared to walk home through any snow!"

Phil chuckled. "You and me both, Mr. Caulder."

Will grabbed his time card, pushed it into the clock, and placed it in one of the slots to the right. "Phil, I'll bet E.B. Horn is the only business left in Boston that still uses these stupid time cards."

Phil chuckled. "You're right about that, Mr. Caulder. This company has old owners who won't change their old business habits."

As one of two bench jewelers, it was his job to check all shipments against the manifest, then lock it up in the vault, and set the alarm system. A guard was posted near the entrance to the vault as an added measure of security. The jewelry store was more concerned with someone forcing their way into the vault, not so much with what was happening inside it. No one would need to access the vault tomorrow. So, they wouldn't realize the stones were gone until sometime Monday. Because Will was working this morning, he wasn't expected back until Monday afternoon. He smiled at the simplicity of his plan. He knew by then it would be too late. *I will be long gone.* He'd already bought a Greyhound ticket to Montreal and would just need an airline ticket to South America. *Warm weather, nice places to live and low expenses. I am so fucking ready!*

He found himself glancing at the clock every few minutes, finding it increasingly difficult to focus on the emerald on his work table. *Where's the damn shipment?* He knew he was not leaving himself much time to make the swap. *It can't be delayed. No diamonds, no meeting. Shit! Will they come looking for me?* He felt sweat start to run down his chest as he heaved a troubled sigh. *There are so many things that can go wrong.*

Just after 11:15 am, the guard appeared at his work bench. "Excuse me. Mr. Caulder? There's a shipment here and you need to sign for delivery."

He jumped out of his chair startling the guard with his uncharacteristic enthusiasm. "Great!" *God, I hate cutting things this close.* He weakly smiled at his unintended pun.

Phil shook his head and mumbled, "You sure do love your job, Mr. Caulder."

Will stretched out his arm. "Lead the way Phil. I'm right behind you." He followed the guard to the delivery entrance.

A stern-looking Brinks delivery man handed Will the padded package. He read the package contents label, then signed the clipboard. Will turned, package under his arm, and headed back to lock up the contents.

The man's booming voice stopped Will in his tracks. "One moment, sir."

Will froze, heart pounding, unable to think why he was being stopped. He slowly turned around. "Yes. Is there a problem?" He could hear the quiver in his voice.

"Yes sir." He pointed at Will's hand. "You have my pen."

Will looked down. He was unaware he still had the pen in his hand. He managed a half-hearted grin. "Oh, sorry about that. Here you go."

He shook his head, a tense smile fixed on his face. He turned and carried the precious package to the over-sized walk-in vault. His fingers trembled as he turned the tumblers and tried to spin the chrome wheel counter-clockwise. *It's still locked.* He stopped for a moment, his sweaty hands resting on the wheel. *Damn it! Get a hold of yourself.* He took a deep breath, wiped his hands on his pants and tried again. He heard a satisfying click. *Yes!* He spun the wheel and pulled open the massive door. *Every time I go in here, it feels like I'm walking into an oversized fucking metal mouth.* He reached to his left and flipped on the lights, illuminating a marble counter, two high-top stools, and a bank of labeled boxes lining the back wall.

He slid onto the seat at the counter, placing the shipment of diamonds in front of him. He was painfully aware a guard was standing just a few feet outside the vault door. He felt his heart thudding painfully in his chest. He placed both hands on the counter and closed his eyes. *I can do this. I still have plenty of time.* He carefully opened the package and unwrapped the tissue from the packets of precious stones. There were ten packets, eight stones in each packet. He counted each packet and then placed the stones on the marble counter. *Eighty beautiful glittering diamonds.* He took a deep satisfying breath. *Mine, all mine.*

He stood up, pulled up his shirt, then slid the money belt down over his hips, stepping out of it and placing it on the counter. He carefully lifted the glass stones out of the four pouches from all around the inside of the money belt. Conversation sounds floated in from jewelers working just outside the vault door. He momentarily stopped to listen to check for anything important going on, then carefully wrapped the glass stones in the tissue from the diamonds, placing them in one of the small drawers inside the vault. He took the diamonds and started to distribute them equally in the lycra pockets around the money belt. His shaking hand accidentally knocked one of the diamonds onto the metal floor. It bounced making multiple distinctive pinging sounds. He froze...one heartbeat, two heartbeats.

A voice floated in from outside the vault as another guard walked toward the vault door. "Hey, butterfingers. Everything all right in there or do I need to stand next to you when you count those diamonds?"

Shit, he can't come in and see what I'm doing. "No problem here! Everything's good." He screwed up his face, trying to think of a witty reply. "That will teach me to go out drinking the night before a workday," he lied. "I should have waited until tonight to tie one on."

The guard chuckled. "You know what they say, Mr. Caulder. Don't do the crime if you can't do the time."

Oh, you'll never know how true. Will waited motionless, acutely aware of his wet shirt clinging to his skin. He heard the sound of receding footsteps, then slowly reached down and picked up the diamond. He waited a moment until he was sure the guard did not return. Then he placed the wayward glittering stone into one of the pouches. Caulder felt around the belt, making sure the Velcro closures on the pockets were secure, then pulled the belt up over his hips and adjusted it around his waist. He carefully tucked in his shirt to hide the bulging belt, then stood up and slowly stepped back from the counter, scanning the interior of the vault. *Once I leave, I'm gone for good.* He stood motionless. *No turning back now.* He took a deep breath and nodded. *This is going to work.* He turned off the light and exited the vault.

Will squinted as he looked up, eyes burning. *Damn I never noticed how bright those lights are.* He turned and leaned with two hands on the massive steel door causing it to slowly close with a resounding thump. He reached up and turned the chrome wheel clockwise one full turn.

He looked over at the guard who was now busy looking through the sports section of the Boston Globe. *He never even looked up when I left the vault. So much for security.* Will made his way down the short corridor to his worktable. *I never remember the stones feeling this heavy when I practiced with the glass ones.* They angrily remind him of their presence with every step he took. *This reminds me of.* He shook his head. *No, not going there.* He glanced at the clock up on the wall making an annoying click, click, click sound, then over to the window at the incessant blaring of car horns and traffic noise on Winter Street.

Will started working, turning his attention to polishing the round-cut emerald in front of him. *This 58-facet cut is a beauty. I'd love to take it with me. Unfortunately, it's for a customer later today.* He shook his head. *Can't be stupid. Got to stick to the plan.* He found himself momentarily lost, staring at the gem's beauty, envisioning himself living in a beautiful hacienda, owning a small business and working with precious stones like these in a tropical South American hideaway.

He looked up from his reverie, turning his eyes to the clock. It was already ten minutes before noon! *Stop daydreaming and start packing up!* He carefully wrapped the emerald, placed it back in its brown envelope, and returned it to the drawer in his table. *I sure am sorry I can't take you with me, you little beauty.*

He scanned the room. There was only one gemologist still working there. He pushed away from the work bench and stopped for a long moment taking a deep breath. *Need to take it slow and casual, just another work day.* He grabbed his jacket and lunch bag and took his time sauntering over to the time clock. He could feel the sharp edges of the stones digging into his skin with every step. He punched out and fumbled trying to place his time card in the slot to the left of the clock. The sudden wailing of a car alarm made him jump.

"Well, you *are* jumpy today, Mr. Caulder. What's got you so spooked?"

Will had forgotten about the guard sitting behind him. *Cool, stay cool. I'm almost home free.* He turned shaking his head. "I don't know why Phil, but it's been a really stressful morning. But, now that I'm done for the day, I know *just* what I need to calm my nerves." He made a slow motion lifting a glass to his lips like he was enjoying a drink.

Phil laughed. "I hear you, Mr. Caulder. I hear you." He shook his head. "I wish *I* was done for the day. Have one for me, will you?"

Will shot him a knowing smile. "Just one? Phil. you must be kidding. I plan to have *way* more than one for you today." He could hear Phil's hearty laugh echo behind him as he left the entry, walking down the grated metal stairs and out onto Winter Street Place.

Chapter 9

Will arrived at the Black Seed Cafe and Grille a few minutes before noon. He shifted from one leg to the other glancing around nervously. Once or twice he saw someone in the crowd walking toward the restaurant and thought it might be Benny. However, they kept walking leaving him increasingly apprehensive and checking his watch. A wiry-looking man, clean shaven with sharp features and a Red Sox baseball hat, wearing a faded blue jacket seemingly appeared out of nowhere. He was carrying a scuffed, but expensive looking brown leather briefcase with two locking brass sliding catches.

"I believe we have some business to conduct over lunch." Will jumped slightly, then nodded. Benny led the way. He opened the brass-handled wood door for Will and then followed him in. They were seated at a secluded table near the back that looked over most of the tables in the restaurant. By habit, Benny sat on the bench seat with his back to the wall. Will took off his jacket and threw it on his lunch bag on an empty chair to his left. Benny slid the briefcase onto the other chair.

A perky, young waitress hurried over to greet them. Benny looked up. "I think we're going to need a little more time before we order."

She tipped the top of her pencil toward him. "Sure. I'll just bring you some water, and you can let me know when you're ready to order."

The waitress dropped off the water and Benny watched her as she moved away to another table. He looked back at Caulder, his face all business. "Okay, I need to see some of the merchandise I'm buying."

Caulder looked around nervously. "You want to look at them here in the restaurant?"

Benny made a face. "No, in my mobile diamond lab parked outside. Jesus H. Christ, Caulder. Do you really think anybody really cares what we're doing? They're all too busy stuffing food in their pie holes." *What did this guy think we were just going to make the swap and walk away? He must be one really dumb shit.*

Will looked left and right, then reached down and pulled up the front of his shirt. He reached in, opened up one of the pouches, and pulled out three round cut diamonds, placing them on a red cloth napkin on the table. Seeing the money belt, Benny made a face. *Shit, a money belt. That's going to complicate things. These better be fucking worth it.* Benny took out a pair of tweezers and picked up the largest gem. He took a jeweler's loupe from his pocket, held it up to his eye and turned the diamond slowly, moving it nearer than farther away from the loupe. Then he picked up and inspected one of the smaller stones, all the while keeping his face passive. *Okay. These are the real fucking deal, high-quality stones, classic cuts, pure color, great clarity.*

"Okay. These all look legit. Put them back in your pouch. The rest of the stones better be as good as these."

Will eyes flashed, anger boiling up. "Yes. They *are* all that good!

Benny looked over at Will's flushed face and smiled. "Jesus! Look buddy, don't go getting your pantyhose in a bunch. You act like you're selling your family heirlooms or something." He shook his head. "The money we agreed on is in the briefcase." Benny nodded to the chair beside him.

Will looked down and pulled the chair closer with his leg. He slid the catches on the briefcase, which released with a satisfying click. He opened the cover just enough to inspect the contents. He stared, wide-eyed at the twenty neatly bundled stacks held in place with a wide elastic strap. He reached in and slid out one stack. He counted one stack with fifty faded green hundred-dollar bills. He returned it and closed the cover. "Okay. It looks like it's all there." He had intended to make a quick transaction and leave, but Benny seemed in the mood for a more elaborate lunch. He called the waitress over, ordering a bottle of Pellegrino and lobster salad for both of them.

Benny beamed at Caulder. "Let me buy you lunch today."

Caulder looked surprised at Benny's sudden generosity. "Ah, sure. I guess." He relaxed and started talking about his work as a bench jeweler. Their lunch arrived and Will continued talking about his work in the jewelry business as he ate. Benny sat feigning interest in Will's description of his jewelry setting techniques. Will demonstrated using an empty water glass as an oversized diamond. "More Pellegrino, Caulder?" Benny held up the bottle.

Caulder looked up momentarily from his diamond setting demonstration and checked his watch. "Ah, just a little. I have an appointment I can't miss. Thanks."

Benny refilled both glasses, deftly pouring the hidden contents of a small vial into Will's glass. Will continued to drink as he talked, surprised that Benny was so interested in the work he did as a bench jeweler. He began to elaborate on the source of the diamonds. Will stopped. He looked up wide-eyed gasping, holding his hand to his belly, as a sudden nightmarish stabbing pain shot through his stomach and began to spread like fire through his abdomen.

Benny hissed, "What the hell is wrong, Caulder?"

Will looked up, his face now creased in deep distress. "Shooting pains in my stomach."

Benny stared at him in mock alarm. "Aw crap. I'll bet it was that damn lobster we ate. I hope I'm not going to be sick too." He lowered his voice. "We better get outside. I think we're starting to attract attention." He threw four twenty-dollar bills on the table to cover lunch and tip. He grabbed Will's jacket and the briefcase, then helped him to a side exit near the back of the restaurant. As they passed by the front of the restaurant, Benny noticed Bull looking down as he hungrily chomped into an overly large sandwich, its contents dripping down his beefy fingers. *I thought I'd managed to lose him. Well, I just hope he doesn't realize we've left for a while.*

He quickly steered Will to the right, heading down Winter Street. Benny shivered, suddenly remembering he had forgotten to take his jacket, but knew it was too late to go back and get it. As they neared Washington Street, he steered Will left into an alley and leaned him against the side of a dumpster. *Christ, I'm freezing my ass off, but business first, the diamonds.* By now, Will was doubled over in agonizing pain, barely able to see, and starting to vomit. Benny started to tug on the money belt, trying to take it off. "Listen, buddy. I need the diamonds. So I'm going to take your money belt off. It'll probably help to relieve the pressure on your stomach."

Will could see Benny still holding the briefcase full of money and was dimly aware through his painful spasms what was about to happen. He started to struggle and turn away from Benny. With great effort he shouted between breathless moans, "No. The money. You can't have it. It's mine! Don't. Stop. Help!"

One of those damn police patrols are going to hear him. "Shut up, Caulder! The cops are going to hear you." This did nothing to quiet Will as he continued a steady stream of loud moans and protestations. Benny shook his head. *No other choice. Tough luck, Caulder.* He reached into his waistband, pulled out a small gun, pressed it against Will's chest and pulled the trigger. There was a muffled 'crack,' and Will fell backwards against the dumpster, sagging to the ground, blood oozing from a blackened hole in his chest.

Benny knelt at Will's feet, struggling to get the money belt off the dying man. *Where's the fucking buckle on this contraption? Great! There isn't any.* Benny realized he was going to have to take it off by pulling it up over Will's head or down over his feet. *Shit. It looks like the easiest way is down over your feet.* First he took off Will's jacket, then he wrestled with the belt, tugging it over Will's hips and pushing it down one side at a time, over his legs and his feet. When it finally came free, Benny was thrown backward and landed with a thump on the trash-littered asphalt. *Can't believe he used a fucking money belt. I knew this was going to be a pain in the ass.*

Benny clumsily pulled the money belt up his legs and around his waist, then put on Will's Patriot's jacket to hide it. He looked down at the lifeless twisted body. "Thanks Caulder for the jacket, and the money." He picked up the briefcase and turned to go. He heard newspapers rustling behind the dumpster. *Shit, I can't believe this! There can't be somebody back there. Can there?* Walking cautiously toward the noise, he took a quick step around the dumpster and pointed the gun in the direction of the sound.

His eyes locked for a moment on a sleepy-eyed street vagrant who had settled down for an afternoon nap in a sea of old newspapers. Benny's eyes narrowed. *I wonder how much that old wino saw?* A grim acknowledgment settled on Benny's face. *Can't chance it.* "Tough luck old man." As he started to squeeze the trigger, he heard voices echo from outside the alley. *What the fuck?* He peered back around the dumpster and froze. A couple had stopped at the entrance to the alley. The old man's raspy voice suddenly rang out. "Please don't kill me!"

The couple turned and stared into the alley. The girl's eyes widened, and she let out a gasp. She saw the crumpled form of the dying jeweler. Benny heard the boyfriend shout, "Go. Find a cop!" He turned and started to cautiously walk toward the body on the ground. *With all police patrols around, it won't take her long to find a cop. I have to get the fuck out of here.* Benny started to point the gun at the boyfriend crouching over the body. The vagrant chose that moment to start crawling away through the litter.

Benny softly swore as he turned and fired at the rustling paper. The sudden noise startled the boyfriend. He looked out toward the street, unsure if he heard a gunshot or a car's engine backfire. He started to stand up. Benny emerged from behind the dumpster and swung his pistol into the side of his startled face, knocking him backward, falling over Will's feet. Benny stood for a moment looking down at the boyfriend, debating. *Out cold, fuck it, time to go.*

Benny emerged from the alley and saw the girlfriend talking to an officer on foot patrol and pointing in his direction. His stomach tightened and he tensed his jaw. He turned, walking briskly away from the alley, resisting the impulse to break into a run. He had planned to return briefly to his apartment and then drive a rental car as fast as possible out of the city and keep driving until he found warm weather. *Don't have time to go back there now. Might be a couple of eyewitnesses who could ID me.*

He reflexively shoved one his hands into a pocket for warmth and felt the loose change, papers, and what felt like a ticket. He pulled it out. *I'll be damned. A greyhound bus ticket.* He squinted to read the date and time. *The date's today, and the departure time is 1:30, in less than,* he looked at his watch, *thirty minutes. What a lucky break. I'll be out of the city before they even start looking for me.* Benny heard, or thought he heard, voices shouting behind him. He put his head down, ignored it and picked up the pace, nearly falling on the snowy sidewalk. *Isn't anything going to stop me now. Thank you, Mr. Caulder. For a loser, you had perfect timing!*

Chapter 10

Bull had just started to put down his glass of beer after washing down a healthy-sized chunk of his pastrami sandwich when he casually turned around to check on Benny and his pasty looking friend. He jumped up and brought the glass down hard on the table, the amber liquid splashing over his hand. Several patrons looked over in alarm as Bull scanned the restaurant with anxious eyes for a sign of Benny. He ran to the hostess station, pushing a couple aside who were in the middle of asking a question. "What happened to the two guys sitting at the back table?" he shouted at the startled hostess.

"Excuse me?"

Bull started to point again with one fat finger toward the back of the restaurant, his face was drawn in a menacing scowl. "Stupid bitch, never mind." He raced out the front door leaving a startled hostess, her hand raised in mid-protest. He stopped and looked left and right. He turned right, walked to the corner, and started to cross Winter street. He stopped halfway. There was some sort of commotion to his right, about fifty yards down the street. He started walking quickly toward a policeman and some bystanders pointing toward an alley on the left. He couldn't be sure, but it looked like Benny's slim figure hurrying away in the distance, still wearing a baseball hat, a different jacket, and carrying a briefcase. A second policeman joined the first and had started to stop pedestrian traffic from approaching from either direction. Bull abruptly stopped and pulled out his phone. He hit a speed dial number, and listened to the electronic sounds of the numbers, dreading the conversation with his boss.

The bartender placed a blue napkin with the Legal Seafood Logo down on the bar followed by a frosted mug filled with Sam Adams. Lou was early for his lunch meeting and had enough time for a quick beer. His cell phone rang. He looked at the caller ID. *Damn. It's Bull. Why the hell is he calling me?* He pushed 'talk'. "This better be good. You're interrupting something important."

"Sorry boss. It looks like Benny's done a runner."

"You *are* with him, of course. Right?"

"Ah. Well, Benny slipped out of the restaurant by a side door. When I saw he left, I chased after him. It looks like he dumped the guy in an alley off Winter Street. He's got the money, and I'm guessing he's got the stones too."

Lou spoke low with a dangerous urgency. "That's fucking great. Where is Benny now?"

"Well, he was walking down Summer Street toward South Station. The cops have blocked off Winter Street. I'm making my way around and heading back towards there now."

"There's a dozen ways he could leave the city from South Station. Check the train platforms and the bus terminals. If you find him, get him to a quiet place and show him what a big mistake he's made, then bring me the money and the diamonds. If he's in a crowd and you can't do that, just stay with him. Check in with me either way." Before Bull could say a word, the line went dead. He picked up the pace and headed for South Station.

Lou stared at the frost sliding down the outside of his glass. He reached over, drank a mouthful and carefully set the mug down on the coaster with the smiling fish logo. He tapped on the bar a few times, then picked up his phone and punched in the number of one of his drug dealers. "Brian. Lou Vitelli. We've got a problem."

53

Chapter 11

Nia surveyed the crime scene. Yellow tape cordoned off the area around the dumpster where the body was found. Winter Street Place was a dead-end alley immediately behind E.B. Horn jewelers. It hosted a dumpster, the random delivery truck, and an occasional homeless vagrant looking for a quiet place to drink, sleep, and defecate in peace. The officer in charge, a heavyset round-faced cop with a strong Boston accent greeted her, pulled out a small notebook, and filled her in on what they had found.

"We have a white male, mid to late thirties, shot once." He pointed to the small pool of blood on the ground. "It looks like the assailant shot the victim at close range. There were no apparent signs of a struggle. Larry, no last name, a vagrant, heard the shooting. He was looking for a place to sleep behind the dumpster. The assailant must have heard noises and walked around to investigate. He would have shot Larry but was interrupted by…" He hesitated, flipping a couple of pages, and consulted his notes again. "Paul Wright and his girlfriend, Susan Graves, who heard his cries for help. The girlfriend alerted the foot patrol while the boyfriend went into the alley to help what he thought were cries from the deceased. The assailant took a shot at Larry who was beating a hasty retreat, but he missed. He then emerged from behind the dumpster and assaulted the startled boyfriend with a pistol to the side of his face. Given the timeframe for these events, I'd say the victim's been dead less than an hour. We have the vagrant and the couple waiting in the back of the ambulance."

Sergeant Burke flipped a few pages back in his notebook. "Oh yeah. There's one more thing that might be connected. One of our guys on foot patrol reported in about 20 minutes ago. He got a call from the hostess at Black Seed Cafe and Grille around the corner on Tremont Street. She reported two men suddenly left the restaurant through a side door. Apparently, one of them was in some distress and seemed to match the description of the victim."

"Thanks, Sergeant."

Will Caulder. A sad smile crossed Nia's face as she approached the body. Police photographers were finishing taking pictures and a second police ambulance stood ready to take the body to the Medical Examiner at the morgue. *I wish I was wrong about my feeling that we'd meet again. Too bad it's under these circumstances.* She turned to the officer in charge. "This man's name is Will Caulder. He worked at E.B. Horn as a bench jeweler."

Sergeant Burke looked at her surprised and cocked his head. "How come you know so much about the vic detective?"

"He was a witness at an unrelated shooting a couple of days ago." She pulled on latex gloves and crouched down next to the body. Caulder lay on his back with his shirt pulled up and his legs bent at the knees. *So, what happened here Will Caulder?* His blue dress shirt was partially pulled up out of his pants and was soaked with blood. *What reason would there be to pull up your shirt unless you had something hidden underneath?* She lifted the shirt and examined the exposed skin on the victim's stomach. A series of slight irregular impressions showed all the way around his waist. *What would cause that? Must have been something you wore next to your skin. Maybe some sort of fanny pack? No. Not a fanny pack, more like a money belt. Pretty old-fashioned thing for you to be wearing. So what were you carrying that would leave marks like that? Money? No. Some kind of jewelry, precious stones with points and sharp edges.*

Nia moved up to inspect the frayed hole ringed with black power just below the pocket. *Shot and killed at close range with a small caliber weapon. You let somebody get that close; you must have known them.* Nia looked down at his black leather shoes, curious only for the wear pattern on the bottom of the right shoe. Instead of the usual wear pattern under the ball of his foot, there was a worn rectangular strip running from under the toes to the arch. But that was no mystery. She saw him walk with a slight limp when he left the pawnshop the other day. Nia stood and briefly looked up at the light snow beginning to fall. She knew this might be just another random, senseless theft and murder. But she also stopped believing in coincidences a long time ago. Nia shook her head. *I need to find out how the events of a few days ago are connected to this murder.* She motioned for the ambulance attendants to take the victim away. Then she radioed the morgue and spoke to Sam Tung, the M.E. on duty. Sam had worked as an M.E. for the city of Boston since graduating from medical school eleven years ago. Most of the detectives liked him for his thoroughness and easy-going personality, a rare combination in a profession that sees only the dark side of humanity.

"Sam, it's Nia. I got a DB on the way, and we need a prelim on him as soon as you can."

"Nia, you tell me all of your cases need prelims ASAP. Why would this one be any different?"

"Sam, you are such a hard ass."

"I know. That's why you like me so much. I remind you of you. We should have it in a few hours."

Nia smiled at her friend's reply. "I'll see you about four, Sam."

Nia walked to the ambulance where a young man in his early twenties was holding hands with a young woman with deep brown eyes. The vagrant was sitting across from them wrapped in a gray blanket holding a steaming cup of coffee.

They all looked up at Nia who quickly introduced herself and proceeded to ask what they knew about the assailant.

Nia took out her notebook and turned to the vagrant. "Larry, can you tell me what happened?"

Given his disheveled appearance, Larry was surprisingly lucid in his recall of events. "I heard this guy talking to another guy, just as I was about to get some sleep. I could tell one of them was in real bad pain. I know. I've been there myself. He was making these loud moaning noises. So, I moved the newspapers to cover my head so I could get some sleep. Everything was quiet for a minute and then I hear, bam! I know a gunshot when I hear it, so I keep quiet so nobody knows I'm there. Then, I hear these odd grunting noises. That's when I said to myself, I don't know what crazy shit is going on, but I'm getting the hell out of here. So, I start crawling toward the back of the alley. Next thing I know I hear footsteps crunching on all the shit on the ground. I turn, and I'm looking at these dark eyes that are squinting, trying to see where I am. Then the bastard points his gun. I start to holler, 'Don't kill me'. He stops, turns back looking toward the street. So, I start crawling away like a madman and then I hear the gun go off. I feel the bullet hit my shoe! Just look at this." Larry excitedly pointed to a ragged hole in the top of his shoe.

"You were very lucky, Larry. Do you remember anything about the man who shot at you? Maybe what he was wearing or what he looked like—his hair color, his height, his build, etc.?"

Larry stroked the patchy beard on his face. "I remember he was wearing a baseball hat, Red Sox I think, and he had these eyes. They were dark and mean. He looked like he wanted to kill me."

Nia turned to the boyfriend. "You probably saved this man's life by going into the alley. Though you could have got yourself killed." The boyfriend shrugged and managed a weak smile. The side of his face was covered with a large square of gauze held in place with two strips of white tape. "Paul, can you tell me what happened from when you walked into the alley?"

"Well, I didn't see much. I went into the alley and had just squatted down, trying to help the man on the ground when I was startled by a loud sound close by. I looked around, thinking it might be a car or truck backfire, and started to stand up. This guy appeared out of nowhere. I just glimpsed this angry face for a split second, incredible pain, and then nothing."

"Can you describe this guy?"

"It all happened in a flash. I remember the guy had dark eyes, maybe brown in color. He was wearing a hat and was clean shaven. I think he might have been about my height."

"Did he say anything before or after he hit you, Paul?"

"If he did, I don't remember it. I know at the time I was really worried he might try to hurt Susan."

"Lucky for her she had gone to find the police. Thanks for your help. The ambulance will take you to the hospital to look at that wound. We'll be in touch." As Nia left the ambulance, she called Sergeant Burke over. "Sergeant, I got a description that could fit half the male population of Boston—wearing a baseball hat, probably Red Sox, dark eyes, maybe brown, clean shaven, and a little taller than the victim or about the same height as the boyfriend. The vic is about five nine or five ten, so the suspect and the boyfriend here are probably about six feet. It's not much, but it's a place to start. Have someone bring some mug shots of the usual suspects over to the hospital and see if Paul can ID any of them."

Nia stayed at the crime scene conferring with two forensic specialists who were methodically combing the area for the bullet fired at the vagrant. She pointed at what looked like recent vomit that had oozed down the side of the dumpster and collected in a pool on the asphalt. "Let's take some samples of that," she pointed to the congealing puddle beside the dumpster, "and get it back to the lab for analysis. It may be connected to our victim." She took out her cell phone and took a series of photos of the area to reference later when she wrote up her report. Nia turned and walked up Winter Street toward Tremont, stopping at the corner. She looked at the front of the restaurant and then back down Winter Street. *Why didn't the perp just let Will go and walk away? Was the guy a liability? Maybe he could ID his assailant? If Caulder had to die, then the nearest place out of view was...there.* She pointed back toward the entrance to the alley.

Nia turned and walked into the Black Seed Grille and Café. The hostess, wearing a tight-fitting Black Seed and Grille t-shirt and sporting a short pony tail, was busy studying a seating chart as Nia walked up to greet her.

She beamed at the detective. "Good afternoon, table for one?"

Nia took out her badge. "I'd like to ask you some questions about the two men who left the restaurant in a hurry earlier today."

"Oh, sure." She hesitated. "I did already talk to an officer about it earlier."

Nia nodded. "I have just a couple of follow-up questions. "Can you describe the man who was helping the guy in distress?"

The hostess screwed up her face in thought. "Ah, as they walked by the door, I saw them for a second through the frosted glass. It looked like he was a little taller than the sick guy. Of course, that sick guy was kind of hunched over like he was in pain."

"Did you notice what the taller man was wearing?"

"Well, I noticed he had on a baseball hat, but he wasn't wearing a jacket." She held up her hand, walked behind the hostess station, and lifted up a faded blue jacket and a soft-sided lunch bag. "The waitress brought these back from their table. She thought he might come back for it."

"That's pretty unlikely. I'll take it, thanks. And I'll need to talk to their waitress as well."

"Sure. Oh, and there was one more thing. Shortly after those two left, another man rushed up demanding to know if they had left the restaurant. Before I had a chance to reply, he swore at me, then stormed out of here. He was pretty steamed at something."

Nia took out the notepad she had just put away. "And can you describe that man?"

The ponytail bobbed. "He was heavyset, short cropped hair and his nose looked kind of flat. It was the kind of guy you would not want to meet in a dark alley, if you know what I mean."

Nia nodded. Her short conversation with the gum chewing waitress added nothing to what she already knew about the assailant. She walked back down Winter Street, slipping under the crime tape, mentally ticking off what she knew as she headed into the deserted alley. *So, Will Caulder worked for E.B. Horn as a bench jeweler and would have had access to a lot of precious stones. Maybe this was an inside job that went horribly wrong. But why would there be muscle watching the exchange at the restaurant unless there's someone else involved in what's going on here. And then there's this jacket and lunch bag.* Nia held up the jacket and checked the two outside pockets. *Nothing but lint. And no inside pockets. Let's see what's in this oversized lunch bag.* Nia unzipped it and peered inside. *There's Caulder's passport, what looks like a few family pictures and a high school photo of a serious looking Will Caulder.* She pushed aside the pictures and pulled out a rabbit foot keychain, letting it swing collecting falling snowflakes. *Guess this wasn't so lucky for you, Will Caulder.* She dropped it back into the bag and pulled out some clothes. *You were not only planning to take a trip but were also traveling light. One t-shirt, one pair of socks, and one change of underwear!* She closed, zipped the top, and held the bag up. *I'd have to say you put together a 'get out of Dodge in a hurry kit'.*

Chapter 12

Benny briefly considered taking a cab to the Greyhound bus station. The bodyguard didn't seem to be tailing him anymore and he could have taken a cab and arrived with plenty of time to spare. But he also knew if the cops had already ID him, he'd be leaving an easy trail for them to follow to South Station. *That would be really stupid.* He glanced at his watch. *Twenty-five minutes to get to the bus terminal. A steady walk shouldn't be more than fifteen.* He knew this would be made easier using two streets in the heart of the city, Summer, and Washington. Sections of both streets were made into a pedestrian-only walkway. And he could follow Summer Street directly to the bus terminal at South Station. As he passed by Macy's Department store, a figure suddenly emerged from a set of triple-glassed doors shouting his name. His fingers instinctively wrapped around the gun handle inside his jacket. He slowed and turned to face the man.

"Hey. What's the hurry, Benny?"

He instantly recognized Officer Jim Hernandez, a beat cop assigned to downtown crossing. His hand inside his pocket relaxed as he replied, "I heard there was a two for one sale at Macy's. But I guess I got some bad information."

"Aw come on. You can do better than that, Benny. What do you have in the briefcase?"

Benny's mind raced. He couldn't afford to let him see what was inside. And if he refused, he'd be detained, and it would be game over. "Ah. Just a bunch of racing forms for Suffolk Downs."

Hernandez gave him a skeptical look. "Really? Well, I have to admit playing the ponies does sound a lot more like you."

Benny fixed an imploring look on his face. "Listen, I'm meeting a lady friend for lunch, and I *really* don't want to be late."

Jim gave him a brief look of disbelief. "A lady friend. You? Well, I suppose you *have* managed to keep a low profile lately, so I guess you can go." He pointed at him. "This time, Benny."

Benny turned and continued down Summer Street. It may have been his imagination, but he thought he heard the radio on Hernandez's jacket, crackle to life. *Shit, I hope that's not about me. There's no way I'm fucking stopping.* He picked up his pace. He looked at his watch. South Station was dead ahead, but it was only a few minutes before the scheduled time of departure. He started to jog toward the bus terminal which was about a hundred yards south of the main entrance. With every step he could feel the diamonds press against his skin. *That fucking money belt is killing me. I got to make that bus.*

Outside South Station, a figure emerged from behind one of the large ornate columns. He pulled out his cell phone and punched in a number.

Vitelli's unmistakably nasal voice answered. "Tell me some good news, Brian."

"Benny just blew by here heading for the bus terminal."

"Finally!" The line went dead.

Bull could see Benny in the distance, running up Atlantic Ave along the side of South Station. Bull stopped and impatiently waited for the light to cross. His cell phone rang. He looked down. It was Vitelli. "Bull, he's heading for the bus terminal."

"I see him. He's almost at the bus terminal. He's not getting away this time." He clicked off his phone.

Benny bounded up the steps. As he reached the top, a gust of wind ripped off his baseball hat and sent it flying down the steps and onto the sidewalk. He turned around to retrieve it and saw the unmistakable hulking figure of Bull in the distance crossing Atlantic Ave, only a few minutes behind him.

Shit. No time to chase after it now. He sprinted for the double doors and pushed his way through. He stopped, leaning on a railing only a second to catch his breath. He spotted the Greyhound bus idling five slots to his left. It had almost finished boarding. He jogged down the boarding area steps, joining the end of the disappearing line. Still breathing heavily, he handed the agent his ticket, and looked back as he climbed onto the bus for any sign of Bull. *Not here yet.* He found an empty seat three-quarters of the way toward the back of the bus. He looked down at the woman who had her face buried in a pillow, already fast asleep. On her lap was a detective novel having murder in the title and a Christmas tree with atomic-symbol ornaments on the cover. *A murder mystery, how fucking appropriate.* She didn't stir when he slipped into his seat, which was just fine with Benny. He slipped down into his seat and kept his hand on the gun, just in case.

The bus driver stood in the aisle and introduced himself as he counted the number of passengers. "My name is John Doherty. I'm going to be your driver, and make sure you all arrive safe and sound in Montreal."

From behind him, Benny heard a passenger exclaim "Montreal! Crap, how the hell did I get on the wrong bus?" A heavy-set man hurriedly squeezed by the driver and bolted off the bus.

John shook his head. "Well, I hope the rest of you are going to Montreal." There was scattered laughter inside the bus.

As John started counting the number of passengers, a man seated two rows in front of Benny got up and impatiently tapped his watch.

"And *when* will we be leaving the terminal?"

John replied with practiced patience. "Well, Mr.?"

"Finch. Norman Finch."

Benny smirked. *I can almost picture the pompous, impatient look on that idiot's face.*

"Well Mr. Finch. As soon as I confirm the number of passengers, and have been cleared by the operations manager, we'll be on our way to Montreal."

Finch had a disgruntled look as he responded, "Well we are already several minutes behind schedule. And I *thought* this company had a good reputation for on-time arrivals!"

John took a deep breath. "We will make every effort to see that you arrive on time, Mr. Finch."

Finch's response was to snort, sit down, and turn away toward the window mumbling "Well I certainly hope so."

When John returned to the driver's seat, he adjusted his inside mirror, allowing him to better monitor what was happening inside the bus. Mr. Finch was now staring straight ahead with narrowed eyes and a grim expression. He had a feeling it wouldn't be the last time he'd be hearing from this passenger.

Bull crossed Atlantic Ave. and sprinted along the sidewalk to the granite stairs leading up to the bus terminal. He threw open the doors, scanning the cavernous space looking for Benny. What he didn't anticipate was that there would be several buses queued up to leave inside the terminal and three or four in the process of unloading. Benny was nowhere in sight. He boarded the closest bus and ran down the aisle checking seats. The bus driver stood up as he passed. "Can I help you?"

Bull, anxious not to make a scene, mumbled, "My friend forgot his wallet, and I'm trying to find him."

The bus driver relaxed. "Oh. Do you know what bus he's on or where he's going?"

"No." Bull knew that sounded odd. "Wait, I think he told me he was headed out of the country."

The driver stopped and checked his clipboard. "Well, I don't have all the buses listed, but it looks like at least two are heading to Canada. You should check bays four and five."

Bull nodded and scrambled off the bus. He jumped onto the bus in bay four and started to walk toward the rear of the bus, scanning the faces of the passengers. He didn't see Benny.

The bus driver stopped him as he turned, halfway down the aisle. "May I help you?"

"My friend forgot his wallet. I'm trying to get it to him before he leaves." There was a roar of exhaust from the next bay as the Greyhound pulled out of the station. "Damn." He charged by the driver, knocking him aside. He leaped off the bus and raced to catch up with the departing bus, hoping to catch a glimpse of Benny in one of the windows, but it was already leaving the station. He stopped, panting heavily. "I can't tell Mr. Vitelli I lost him again. Maybe he's not on that bus." He quickly checked the remaining buses without any luck. He took out his phone and steeled himself for the phone call he dreaded making. He hit one of the speed dial numbers.

Lou was still sitting at the bar watching the snow begin to obscure the view of Boston Harbor when he felt the phone vibrate in his pocket. "Bull, tell me you have good news about our friend."

Bull grimaced. "Sorry boss. The bus left the station before I could get to it." He heard the sound of a fist hitting something hard.

"Damn. Well, what *can* you tell me?"

"He's got to be on the Greyhound bus, and it's headed for Montreal."

Lou's face turned dark and menacing. "Out of the country. That's just fucking great." He clicked off the phone mumbling, "What good is muscle if he can't find his way out of a fucking paper bag?" He checked on his phone, details about Greyhound service to Canada from Boston. Apparently the bus made one short stop in a mall, in Lebanon, NH before continuing through Vermont on its way to Montreal. Lou looked back up at the snow now pummeling the plate glass window at back of the bar. "Okay. That's where we'll catch that little two-timing weasel. He'll disappear if he makes it to the border." He pounded the bar again. "I'm not going to let that happen." He swiveled on his bar stool, looking grim-faced at his bodyguard. "Right Rocco?"

Rocco nodded solemnly. "Right boss."

Lou pointed at his bodyguard. "You and I are going for a little ride." Vitelli hated to get directly involved in the seedier side of his business, but he couldn't let Benny get away with his money *and* the diamonds. "And when we find Mr. Benjamin Penny, there'll be some business that I'm going to let you personally take care of for me."

Chapter 13

Nia looked up the number for the manager of E.B. Horn. "Mr. Resnick? This is Detective D'Amato of the Boston Police. I'm sorry to inform you that one of your employees, Will Caulder, was fatally shot outside the rear of your store on Winter Street Place."

"What? No! Who is this again? Is this some sort of prank?"

"No, Mr. Resnick. This is not a prank. We believe Mr. Caulder may have been involved in the theft of some jewelry from your store sometime this morning."

"That's impossible, detective. We have strict check-out protocols for all our employees and armed security guards at all the entrances.

"Well, Mr. Resnick, I hope that I'm wrong, but we are going to need to find out if anything is missing. Could you please have your security people meet me at the front of the store?"

"Of course. I'll need to check the authenticity of this call with the Boston Police before you arrive."

"Yes. Of course. I look forward to seeing you in about fifteen minutes. Thank you."

Nia's phone rang a few minutes later. "D'Amato. Deputy Commander Flynn. What's the status of your homicide investigation?"

"Sir, I'm going to be checking out a possible robbery connection at E.B. Horn with the dead man who worked there. There's evidence to suggest that this was some sort of deal gone bad. I'm going there now to have them check their inventory."

"Good. Keep me informed on your progress, detective."

"Yes, sir." The line went dead. She looked at the receiver, her face betraying her annoyance. *Still keeping close tabs on me, Commander.* She shook her head. *Some things never seem to change.*

Nia found Sergeant Burke still at the crime scene, and together they walked to E.B. Horn. A confident-looking manager left his office flanked by two security guards and moved around the display cases to meet her. Nia showed him her identification. "Thank you, detective. You can't be too careful these days. I'm the store manager, Macy Resnick. We have checked Will Caulder's work station, and everything seems to be in order. I feel relieved you were mistaken about the robbery. I assure you we vet our employees quite thoroughly. Mr. Caulder was one of our most skilled and dedicated bench jewelers. Why just yesterday he offered to work this morning in place of a sick employee." He stopped and moved a hand to his lips. "Oh dear. If he hadn't come to work today, he might still be alive."

Nia nodded. "Well thank you for checking, Mr. Resnick." She started to leave but stopped and turned. "So, was there anything else that Mr. Caulder might have worked with, perhaps not at his work station, that might be missing?" Mr. Resnick looked up thinking and shook his head. "No. It's one of the security protocols we use to limit employee access to precious jewels."

D'Amato nodded, then noticed one of the security guards looking troubled and trying to decide something. Nia looked over at him. "Yes, sir? Do you have some information you'd like to add?"

The guard hesitated, looked quickly over at Mr. Resnick, then back at Nia. "Well, I stood guard outside the vault while Mr. Caulder checked in an order of diamonds that arrived late this morning."

The manager's eyes went wide with shock, and he hit his head with his hand. "I am *so* sorry. Today was a madhouse and we don't get regular Saturday shipments of diamonds. I completely forgot there was one due for delivery today."

"What was the value of the diamonds, Mr. Resnick?

He hesitated a moment looking up. "I believe the resale value was about two million dollars.

"Could you check to make sure they are still in the vault, please?"

"Oh, yes. Of course." Several minutes passed. Mr. Resnick returned looking pale and worried. "When I first quickly checked the number of stones, they were all present and accounted for. But something didn't look quite right. So, I got a jeweler's loupe and checked several of the stones." He lifted his hands and shook his head. "Detective, they are all fake. They're made of glass." He looked away and then back at Nia. "You said Mr. Caulder was dead. Do you *have* the diamonds?"

Nia shook her head. "No, we don't. Mr. Resnick, you mentioned that Will Caulder was a skilled and dedicated employee. But can you tell me more about his personal life? Did he have any close friends either here or outside of work?

The manager stopped a moment considering the question. "Well, I think it's fair to say he was something of a loner. He usually ate lunch alone, and I don't recall him ever talking about his social life outside of work. He was single, as far as I know. And I don't believe he ever attended any of E.B. Horn's holiday or retirement parties. However, his time management skills were impeccable. He was never late for work, always came back on time from lunch, and almost never took a day off for any reason." He lifted a hand to his lips. "That's what makes this theft all the more puzzling."

Nia nodded. "Thanks, Mr. Resnick. Please leave the glass stones where they are. We'll have someone from the criminal investigation division come down and take statements and dust for prints to determine if Mr. Caulder acted alone."

Mr. Resnick opened his mouth then closed it. He looked down, almost talking to himself. "He may not have acted alone. Oh, that would be most troubling if someone else was involved." He turned and walked back into his office, still shaking his head.

Chapter 14

Light snow had already begun to fall as the Greyhound bus emerged from the Central Artery, onto the Zakim Bridge. If Benny hadn't been so anxious to get out of the city, he might have noted the white harp-style cables supporting the elevated north-south roadway over the Charles River. Route 3/93 through Boston was always chaotic with frenzied drivers in a hurry to get to their destination. Adding precipitation to the mix usually meant that heavy traffic would become a frustrating, stressful, stop-and-go nightmare. Today was no different. They inched along the highway in small stops and starts. After 30 minutes, they weren't more than a handful of miles outside of the city. John kept expecting Finch's round disgruntled face to appear at any moment. He wasn't disappointed for long.

An angry bark issued from a man in the aisle just behind the driver. "Can't you find any way around all this mess?"

John tightened his hands on the wheel and took a deep breath before responding. "I've been monitoring road reports since before we left the city, Mr. Finch. All the roads around the city are in gridlock and traffic is at a standstill. Route 93 North is still the shortest and safest route out of the city."

John heard a quick snort behind him. "I can't believe this!"

"*Mr. Finch.* Please return to your seat. It's not safe to be standing while the bus is in motion."

John heard a receding voice respond. "Well, I don't see much motion going on here." A few of the passengers chuckled at his retort.

An amused look lit up Benny's face as he stared out at the shifting veils of increasingly heavy snow. *I like it. Having an angry passenger distracts any attention away from me.* For the first time since the robbery and murder, he felt himself relax as the bus pushed inexorably further North, putting more distance between him and the crime scene.

***

Vitelli and Rocco were inching along the Central Artery, stuck in the same massive traffic jam, no more than fifteen minutes behind the Greyhound bus. The cherry red Porsche 911 was a car Vitelli drove to impress others. It was fast, flashy and terrible in the snow because of its rear engine design. Every time Vitelli saw any opening in a lane in the traffic ahead, he would give it too much gas and wind up fish-tailing, going nowhere, and fighting to regain control. Rocco sat wide-eyed, gripping the edges of the passenger seat, wishing someone, actually almost anyone else, was behind the wheel. After they had been on the road for about an hour, Rocco leaned forward staring intently through the driving snow. "Boss, it looks like that might be a bus up ahead in the center lane."

Vitelli nodded and changed lanes to get close enough to see if it was the Greyhound. "Yes! I've got you now you double-crossing bastard. Oh, revenge will be sweet. And I want it to be slow and very painful" He looked over at Rocco flashing an angry grimace.

Rocco nodded. "You got it boss, slow with lots of pain."

Vitelli slowed down, trying to move directly behind the bus, but there was another car blocking the lane. He made a disgruntled noise, having no choice but to let the Greyhound get a few car lengths ahead before trying to ease to the right between two cars. A horn blared in protest. "Can you believe all these asshole drivers out on the road?" He looked to his right. "Get off the road if you don't like how I drive, you fucking jerk." Rocco had closed his eyes tightly during the maneuver. He glanced to his right and caught his breath, seeing how close Vitelli had come to hitting the other car. He rolled his eyes, hoping his boss wouldn't notice.

***

The bus started to pick up more speed as traffic thinned and it approached the Massachusetts/New Hampshire border. Visibility out the large front windows of the Greyhound was becoming increasingly difficult as the wipers struggled to keep up with steady sheets of driving snow. Benny pushed up the sleeve of his jacket and glanced at his watch. *Two forty-five. It's been almost an hour and a half since we left.* He smiled, picturing a furious Lou Vitelli berating his bodyguard for losing him. He wondered what else he would do, beyond yelling, to punish them. *I'm glad I'm out of his reach; don't want to think about what he'd do to me. That sadistic bastard wouldn't want it to be quick.* He settled into his seat, made sure the briefcase was secured between his feet, and closed his eyes for what he hoped would be a short, uneventful trip.

Chapter 15

Nia drove by the Shubert and Wang in Boston's theatre district on lower Tremont Street and then by overpriced parking garages and parking lots. Just beyond were high-end apartments on both sides that were part of some recent urban renewal project, mostly affordable by individuals with six-figure salaries. The new steel, brick and triple glazed window facades screamed, 'You're going to need some serious money if you want to live here.' Nia smiled, knowing they were also probably expensively decorated inside. She wondered how long it would take her to afford to live in one of those fancy apartments on a cop's salary. *Keep dreaming.*

After crossing over Mass. Ave, the look of the neighborhoods deteriorated quickly. The cold white frosting coating the buildings hid layers of ugly reality: mostly crumbling neglected facades and minimally habitable living conditions in overcrowded quarters. This felt closer to the Boston Nia knew and grew up in. It was populated by folks who were proud but often frightened and struggling to survive. They were just trying to keep body and soul together to make it alive to the next day. Many of them were angry and bitter, feeling alienated from a city that didn't seem to give a shit about them. They were mostly resigned to where they ended up, left behind by the false promise of an American dream.

Nia heaved a depressed sigh as she looked out the cruiser window. *And then there's the police. Some days it feels like I'm shoveling shit against the tide. I enforce laws, catch bad guys, protect the innocent and those trying to do the right thing. But I also get to watch things break down and unravel. I see the poverty, the racism, the discrimination and hatred that eats away at people leaving them vulnerable and angry.* She drove by a street walker leaning into the passenger window of a silver Mercedes. *Everywhere I look I see the struggles between those having power and control and those who want it, are used by it, or are desperately trying to stay out of the way. And the violence that inevitably follows almost always involves some combination of money, sex, drugs or dysfunctional relationships.* She looked up at the collection of buildings that were part of Boston Medical Center. *Thank God I'm finally here. I hate thinking about all this shit.*

She pulled into one of the reserved parking spaces near the back of the hospital complex. *I hope Sam has some good news for me.* Nia hated the smell of alcohol that always seemed to greet her as she entered the cavernous room that was part of the morgue at Boston Medical Center.

Sam welcomed Nia by pulling down the sheet covering Will Caulder's face. "Here is our unfortunate victim, detective. A lot of this you already know. His name is Will Caulder, occupation—bench jeweler with E.B. Horn jewelers. He's 70 inches in height, one leg a half inch shorter than the other probably causing a slight limp."

Nia impatiently interrupted, "I know that's all important, Sam. But did you find anything out of the ordinary, suspicious fibers, toxicology screen results, name of his killer in his shirt pocket, etc.?"

He looked up and laughed. "Yes, wouldn't that be a nice change of pace. But, there *are* a couple of things that might interest you." Sam walked over to his desk and picked up a small clear evidence bag. "Mr. Caulder had a receipt from Greyhound for $62.50 that was folded in the watch pocket of his pants. It was dated yesterday, December 10th." He looked up as he handed her the receipt. "Nope, we didn't find any ticket in his pockets." He put the bag down and picked up a clipboard. He had lunch about four hours ago...lobster, a Romaine salad, and sparkling water. Most of the meal was undigested indicating that he was killed less than thirty minutes after he ate. Oh, and there was one curious finding. Although death was the result of a gunshot wound made by a 32-caliber pistol at point blank range to the heart, I found evidence that he had been poisoned. It was probably something he ate or drank during the meal. It was a particularly nasty, fast acting acid causing gastroenteritis. This resulted in a burning of the stomach lining causing small perforations. It would have been enough to incapacitate him with violent stomach cramps, but not enough to kill him.

Nia cocked her head, looked puzzled. "So, first, he gets poisoned during a meal by his assailant, so, I have to assume they knew each other." Nia looked at Sam, then started pacing up and down in the lab. "We know that Will Caulder had just stolen diamonds from E.B. Horn. So, maybe he was meeting the buyer for lunch and they planned to exchange the jewels for money. But for a minute, let's assume the buyer had other ideas. He intended to rip Caulder off and keep the diamonds *and* the money. He poisons him, then a little later, he shoots him." Nia stopped, looking at Sam. "If he was incapacitated with poison, why bother shooting him? Why not just leave him in the alley? Was the killer afraid if Caulder lived and realized he was double-crossed that he might later ID him?"

Sam turned and looked down at the waxy, white-faced corpse. "Well, all I know is that he would have started making one hell of a lot of noise with his stomach being burned full of small holes. So the explanation you're looking for might be something a lot simpler. But fortunately, that's why they pay you," he pointed at Nia, "the big bucks to figure out stuff like that, detective."

"Big bucks, yeah, I wish," Nia replied smiling. "Thanks for the quick turn-around, Sam, and for letting me bounce ideas off you." He bowed but said nothing as she turned and left the morgue. She knew from experience that the Greyhound receipt for a cash transaction with no other information just might be a complete waste of time. *And now I get to visit one of the high points of any day, the bus terminal at South Station.*

Chapter 16

The bus terminal, which hosted several bus lines including Greyhound, was about one hundred yards away from the front entrance to South Station. Any time of day or night you could find an assortment of vagrants, streetwalkers, runaways, and wide-eyed tourists, sitting or standing along the granite steps out front, or impatiently waiting outside or just inside the multi-storied steel and glass building. Nia pulled up next to the curb and took a deep breath, looking at the bustling tide of humanity, most eager to get somewhere and a few shabbily dressed solitary figures working the crowd not planning to go anywhere. *Chaotic places like this always make me feel uneasy.* Nia frowned. She knew that any situation over which she had little control made her feel that way. She closed the car door and heard a familiar gravelly voice coming from a slightly stooped figure hovering at the edge of the crowd.

"Hey, detective. Got a cigarette?"

Nia smiled and shook her head. She considered the once attractive, heavily made-up blonde emerging from the building's shadow. "Linda, you know those things will kill you?"

In a raspy voice she replied, "Kill me? You know, detective, there's a lot of things worse than cigarettes that can kill me. I got bills to pay. And you should know I'll be in *worse* shape if I don't pay what I owe."

Nia nodded. "I think the last time I saw you, you looked like hell. You needed stitches and a shot of penicillin at Boston Medical Center."

She studied the battered-looking woman who turned to avoid her steady gaze. "Why don't you ditch that scum ball pimp?"

"Ah. Fucking easy for you to say, detective, not so easy for me to do."

She gave Linda an exasperated look, shook her head then turned and headed for the entrance. A frantic rush of humanity and steady buzz of conversation assaulted her senses as she walked through the reinforced steel and glass doors. She fought her way like a salmon swimming upstream, through a steady surge of pushing, harried commuters, to the supervisor's office.

Nia was greeted at the door by Leroy Yazbek, a middle-aged black man with a close-cropped fringe of white hair encircling his head.

Nia reached out and shook his hand. "Mr. Yazbek, we're trying to track down a ticket sale as part of a murder investigation." Nia handed him the cash receipt. He walked back and stood behind his desk. He ran his finger down a pricing sheet. "That Greyhound receipt amount matches the cost of a one-way ticket to Montreal, Canada on either Saturday or Sunday.

Nia put her hands on his desk. "And how often does Greyhound go to Canada?"

Yazbek turned around and lifted a clipboard off a board behind him. He flipped through several pages. "Let's see. It looks like it makes one trip every day except Saturday. Today it makes two trips."

"And what time does the bus leave today?"

He twisted around in his seat, squinting at the schedule on the wall. "Well, one left this morning at 8:20 and the second one," he ran his finger down the schedule, "already left. "It was scheduled to leave at 1:30 pm."

"Mr. Yazbek, could I see your passenger list for that run?

"Sure. You know, it won't have this person's name." He held up the receipt. "They paid cash and purchased an open ticket for any of our weekend Montreal runs. Unfortunately, this doesn't show the ticket number. So we have no way of knowing if the ticket was used."

"The name doesn't matter since we know the man who bought it is dead. It would be helpful to know if there was a ticket bought for this run, that *wasn't* used today."

"*That* I can tell you. Just give me a minute." He reached over and pushed an intercom button. "Marge, could you bring in the transaction sheet for the 676 to Montreal? Thanks."

"Mr. Yazbek, when is that bus due to arrive in Montreal?

He twisted around in his seat again, squinting at the schedule on the wall, looked at his watch, then looked up like he was reading something off the ceiling. "Let's see. Usually the driver takes 93 north out of Boston to route 89 north through Vermont and into Canada, then changes to route 35 and finally to route 10. So it's almost 4:45 pm and he's scheduled to arrive about 7:45 pm with one short stop in Lebanon, New Hampshire. Of course, given today's weather and the lousy traffic conditions, his arrival time is anybody's guess." *Damn. Once the passengers get off the bus, our suspect will be history. If he decided to use that ticket to get out of town today.*

A few minutes later, Marge entered the office with the passenger list. Yazbek scanned the sheet, then handed the list to Nia. "As you can see there were thirty-four passengers on the bus. Fourteen paid cash. And there are check marks by every name, meaning every cash customer showed up and boarded the bus."

Nia looked at the list. She knew that the suspect could have used the ticket today, or it could be for another one of the weekend runs to Montreal. There were names for eight women and twelve men who used a credit card. There were fourteen paying cash who held a numbered ticket that matched a number on a Greyhound's cash customer list. If the suspect *was* one of those passengers, he'd probably be really anxious to leave town. She looked up at Yazbek. "Who collects tickets from the passengers?"

"The agent at the gate collects the tickets and then the driver does a head count before he leaves to make sure the numbers match."

"I'd like to talk to the gate agent on the off chance they might remember something about one of the cash-paying customers."

Yazbek shrugged. "Good luck with that. With the number of folks passing through here every day, I'd be surprised if they remember anything, but I'll take you to the agent."

Nia tapped on the glass-fronted ticket booth, drawing the attention of the agent who was busy sorting tickets into piles. She held up her badge. "Excuse me. Detective D'Amato. I'd like to ask you some questions about one of the passengers earlier today."

The agent leaned closer, squinting to look at the badge, then leaned back and gave her an irritated look. "Okay, detective." He removed the block from the ticket tray at the bottom of the window.

"Do you remember anything suspicious about any of the customers boarding the 676 Greyhound run to Montreal this afternoon?"

"*Detective* D'Amato," he began, adding sarcastic emphasis to the first word. "I take tickets from hundreds of folks every day. After a while, all the faces look the same to me."

"This would be someone particularly anxious to board the bus."

The agent started to shake his head, then stopped, hesitating. "Well, there *was* this *one* guy who was really impatient, obnoxious really. He kept looking at his watch and he almost threw his ticket at me in his rush to board the bus."

Nia took out a notebook. "And do you remember what this man looked like?"

The agent looked up, thinking. "He was about my height, maybe six feet, middle-aged, and had on this winter jacket. I think it was mostly gray with a different color up on the shoulders. Oh yeah, and he was carrying some kind of a bag.

Our suspect wasn't wearing a jacket. Did he have time to grab one before boarding a bus? "Was he wearing anything on his head?"

The gate agent screwed up his face thinking. "Maybe. But, I don't really remember whether he was wearing a hat."

Nia nodded, closing her notebook. "Thank you. You've been very helpful."

Nia turned to speak to Yazbek who had a hand in the air and a puzzled look on his face. "I'm surprised the gate agent remembered that man so clearly."

Nia nodded. *And, I'm surprised the passenger was acting so obnoxious. Why would he do that and call attention to himself?* "Would you get in touch with the bus driver and ask him to contact me when it's safe, so I can question him about his passengers?"

Yazbek nodded, a look of concern crossing his face. "Detective, should we be concerned about the safety of our passengers?"

"Mr. Yazbek, at this point we are looking for a person of interest who may not even be on that bus. I don't want to cause undue alarm. If the situation changes, the safety of the passengers will be our top priority. I appreciate all your help today. Here, please take my card." Nia checked her watch as she left his office. She knew that the bus wouldn't be arriving in Montreal for a few more hours. And now she had a better idea what this obnoxious passenger looked like who might be the suspect. She hoped to find out more from the bus driver. She shook her head. *That's a lot of maybes. And if that ticket was not for today, I guess I'll be back here before boarding time tomorrow.*

Chapter 17

Nia left the bus terminal and stopped short. There was a group of bystanders standing in a circle off to the side of the entrance. *Wasn't that where Linda was standing?* She changed direction and hurried over, reaching for her badge. "Police, please stand aside." People were standing in twos and threes around a figure lying on the ground. Nia pushed through the knot of onlookers. A man was hunched over a body, Linda, lying on her back. He had his hand pressed over her abdomen, dark red splotches seeping out in all directions. A bloody knife lay on the ground a few feet from her head.

Nia knelt down. "Linda! What the hell happened?" She reached out, gently turning her head.

Linda raised her eyes and tried to give Nia a slight shrug. She breathlessly whispered, "Told you, detective. Got bills to pay."

In the distance could be heard the scream of police sirens. Nia turned to the man helping Linda. His face was ashen, his eyes glassy with shock. "Can you tell me what happened, sir?"

"I don't know." He stopped, his breathing shallow. "I was heading for the bus terminal. Then just ahead of me I saw this lady staggering backward and clutching her stomach. A man wearing a flashy lime green jacket and a flat looking hat, looked like he had just pushed her away. Then he hurried off, back toward the main entrance of South Station. I didn't get a look at his face though. She collapsed onto the ground and started moaning. So, I rushed over and called the police and told them we needed an ambulance. Then I sat down to see if I could help her." He looked down at the blood oozing from under his hand. "But lady, I'm no doctor."

Nia put a hand on his shoulder. "What's your name?"

A scared face looked up at her. "Robert. Robert Thometz."

Robert, you're doing a lot more than most people would. Thank you for staying here and trying to help her."

He looked at her and nodded. "I've never seen anyone." His voice caught and he couldn't continue.

Nia took a deep breath. "I understand. And it doesn't get any easier." Nia leaned over and touched Linda's forehead. "You hang in there, Linda. It's not over till the fat lady sings. And she's not singing now." *Okay, that sounds pretty lame.* She slowly stood, still looking down at the crumpled figure on the ground. She turned to the milling crowd. "Did any of you see what happened?" There was a lot of head shaking and people edging away. She waited for the police to arrive, filling them in on what little she knew before heading back to the precinct station. *Always seems to end this way. Is there only one way out?*

Before pulling away from the curb, she sat, momentarily lost in thought. The adrenaline-inducing manic energy of a crime scene was always followed by the depressing weight of reality in human cost of pain, suffering and lives lost. Sitting in the stillness of her cruiser, one hand too tightly gripping the wheel, she was keenly aware of the bitter taste of frustration. *Some days it seems malice, greed, and death slithers into every corner of this city.* She shook her head in a futile attempt to shake the cold, angry feeling that had settled over her like a damp wool blanket. *It's not all bad. I know there are also some good ones who stop and try to help, try to make things better.*

She started the car and pulled away from the curb with squealing tires. She shook her head. *I really didn't mean to do that. Is this all because Linda got stabbed?* Nia thought about all the violence in her job, wondering who would be there to stand up and protect all the scared, beat up and beat down women who are used and abused all across this city. *The police?* She knew what would happen this time. *Those lazy asses in vice will only pretend to give two shits about a prostitute like Linda.* She knew that even when the police did pursue the perp in those cases involving violence against women, the victim was often too scared to identify the scumbag who did it. She shook her head. *I know what it feels like to be really scared. Enough! Can't change any of that shit. Focus on who killed Caulder.* Nia rounded the corner onto Melina Cass Boulevard sharper than she intended, causing two startled pedestrians to jump back away from the curb, giving her dirty looks.

Part 2: Inn Trouble

Chapter 18

The Vermont Inn, a red converted farmhouse built in the 1840's, consisting of a series of additions stacked end to end, sat nestled at the foot of the thirty-two-hundred-foot Blue Ridge Mountain in Central Vermont. In the 1930's, George Silver and his son converted the farmhouse into a stopping place for transients. It passed through a succession of hands as a ski lodge and eventually as an inn with a year-round restaurant.

The first time that Bill and Megan King visited the Vermont Inn on vacation, they loved everything about it. The rooms were lovingly filled with antiques, bright puffy quilts, hand painted pictures of the Vermont countryside and sprigs of dried aromatic flowers. A small carafe of cream sherry sat waiting on the dresser to greet them. A common sitting room area hosted an overstuffed green checkered sofa with a matching love seat. A red night-shirted teddy sat on top of the sofa looking down at a massive light pine coffee table filled with bowls of fresh fruit, and carafes of hot cider and hot chocolate. A large scrapbook lay open nearby filled with pictures of the inn and its staff as well as letters from former guests.

Walking to the dining room they passed through a set of double doors and a lounge scattered with small tables and leather chairs. A Vermont Castings wood stove sat nestled on a slate floor in one corner facing a cherry wood topped bar. The dining room was paneled with knotty pine darkened by age. A wall of picture windows looked out on a sloping field nestled at the foot of some of the lower hills in the Killington mountain range. On the opposite wall, a fieldstone fireplace pulsed with heat on wintry evenings, orange flames darting from beneath a pile of seasoned maple logs.

Bill was intrigued by the idea of owning and running an inn ever since they stayed at the Rabbit Hill Inn on vacation in northern Vermont. Though initially skeptical about whether they had the background to successfully run an inn, Megan admitted she was interested and willing to discuss the idea. She knew they were both ready for a change of career, and an inn seemed to offer a refreshing, if not somewhat daunting, change. Megan was friendly and outgoing, working every day with families in distress in her job as social worker. Bill managed complex financial transactions as a stockbroker and was a wiz with managing budgets.

Bill and Megan spent several weeks discussing the pros and cons of owning an inn. Bill was ready to tackle the career change and charge headlong without any more delay. But Megan continued to have nagging doubts about the risks involved in putting everything they owned, as well as their future financial survival on the success of running a business they knew very little about. She reasoned that least their current jobs, though stressful and at times tedious, offered a secure income stream. The inn offered an exciting change of lifestyle and a lot of unanswered questions. Bill became impatient with Megan's resistance, and began to press her about buying an inn. At the end of a long tiring week at work, they agreed that they would make a final decision that evening after dinner.

The children had gone to bed and Bill poured them both a healthy glass of their favorite cabernet. Megan followed him into the living room, sitting across from him. Megan raised her glass. "To us. Whatever we decide, whatever comes next, it will always be us, doing it together."

Bill nodded once and raised his glass. "To us and to our future together."

They both took a sip and fell silent. It stretched into an uncomfortable silence. Bill finally looked over at Megan with wrinkled brow and spoke first. "We've been back and forth with this idea of buying an inn and have spent a lot of time kicking it around and well, you know how I feel about it, Megs.

"I know. I'm sorry I'm being so indecisive. I guess I'm worried about all the things we don't know." *And that includes having to work every day with this driven, intense side of you.*

"You're right. We've made lists of all the things we do know, the pros and cons of taking this really big step. We know there's some things we can't resolve unless, until, we actually buy an inn. You know that I think it's a good idea. So what can I do to help you with making this decision?"

Megan shrugged. "Maybe it's just that there's a lot of unknowns. And it scares me, at least as much as I'm excited about the idea of owning an inn."

Bill reached out his hand and Megan squeezed it. "You know together we can do anything. So what do you say, Megs. Are you ready to take the leap with me, partner?"

Chapter 19

When Megan sat down with Molly and Sarah and talked to them about their plans to buy an inn, they were surprised, unhappy, and full of questions. Sarah, being the oldest, took the lead, blurting out, "No. We can't leave all our friends, Mom!" Molly nodded in agreement, crossing her arms, an angry pouting look on her face.

Megan nodded sympathetically. "Well first, we're not going anywhere for a while. We have to visit a lot of different inns and find out all the fun things that you can do there."

Sarah looked over at Molly. "Well, we do like *visiting* inns and doing fun things, but we're *not* moving!"

Megan nodded. "Okay. First we are just going to visit and have some fun. Now, who's up for a little snack?" She followed the chorus of *me's* into the kitchen.

Bill and Megan attended a three-day innkeeper seminar together. The first day focused on learning the basics of running an inn. The second day focused on the details of different business models and software that helped you track income and expenses. And the last day covered how to find, buy, and finance your dream inn. After the seminar ended, they drew up a priority list of 'must haves' and began the search for their 'dream' inn. They visited several perfect sounding inns for sale over the next few months that turned out to be 'handyman's specials'...a realtor's code word for a property in need of serious rehabilitation. After each visit, they spent hours discussing what they found, but none really felt like a place they could call home.

They began to feel discouraged that they would ever find a place that they could afford and had all of the things they really wanted. Megan had just opened one of their favorite websites listing inns for sale when she saw it. Their favorite inn, the Vermont Inn had just been listed for sale. They headed out almost immediately to see it. They chatted with the owners about all the changes made over the past several years as they walked through the rooms. They both felt a growing excitement. They knew that this was the inn they wanted. It was perfect...a two-story inn on five acres in central Vermont. It was close to both Pico Mountain and Killington ski resort and had been hosting travelers for over 80 years. It would only need minor renovations and already had a regular clientele and a restaurant that had won several culinary awards. The rooms were tastefully decorated and located on two levels. They varied in size to accommodate from one guest to a family of five. Another feature they loved was that there were separate innkeeper accommodations housed under the same roof.

As they left the inn and headed to her parent's home in nearby Proctor, Megan turned to Bill excited, but clearly worried that they wouldn't be able to afford it. "Bill, you know how much I love that inn. It's got everything on our 'must have' list. But their asking price is way more than we budgeted. I don't even want to think about the size of our monthly payments."

Bill's face twisted into a determined mask with narrowed eyes. "Yeah. I'm working on that, hon. But this is the one. There's been nothing else that comes close." He stared ahead, eyes unfocused speaking slowly. "It's perfect. I'm sure we can find a way to swing it."

Megan turned away, watching a steady blur of trees slip by her window. *He's so determined to go through with this, even if we really can't afford it.*

It took everything they could borrow and scrape together to get a mortgage, but by mid-August, they were the proud new owners of the Vermont Inn. They set opening day for Labor Day weekend. This gave them almost three weeks to make whatever changes or improvements to the inn on their tight budget. They gave most of the staff two weeks off and convinced the handyman Ted, a former Navy seal and carpenter, who had planned to retire when the inn was sold, to stay on for a while and help them with renovations. He agreed on condition that it would just be until they got through the winter months and into the typically slow period in early spring. Bill and Megan worked eighteen-hour days and would fall into bed exhausted, only to do it all over again the next day.

The children stayed with their grandparents for a two-week 'vacation'. They would come to the inn almost every day to play, ask an endless series of questions, and generally slow down any work that was going on. Megan felt increasingly guilty about the amount of time the inn was taking away from her children. She looked over at Bill, who initially seemed happy to see them but would then send them away, getting annoyed when he felt he needed to get back to work. *I wonder if that means that this will be the new normal. Great to see you kids, now go and play. Maybe it's one of those unknowns we talked about.* She gave her head a small shake, turning back to the blackened brick, accidentally wiping soot on her forehead from the fireplace she was cleaning.

Chapter 20

The inn had already started accepting reservations for Labor Day weekend as soon as they passed papers making the purchase official. When some of the staff returned a couple of days before the opening, thirteen of the nineteen rooms were already booked. Each day Bill would make himself a 'to do' list and inevitably a number of unfinished items would roll over to the next day. With one day left before the opening, Bill resigned himself to not getting everything done. He took out his frustration on everyone, especially Megan. "How's it coming with replacing those faded pictures that are up in the dining room, Megs?"

She grimaced, shaking her head. "Really slow. I wanted the pictures we use in the dining room to look like they all go together. But going through the ones we ordered, I'm having trouble finding five that I like."

Bill's brow creased and he gave his head a small shake. "We just need to get pictures up to cover the spots where the old ones were. It doesn't really matter which ones. We can always replace them later when we have more time."

Megan bit her lower lip. "I think it's important that the dining room look like we spent some time on tastefully decorating it. I don't want it to look like a cheap diner where someone just threw up some random pictures on the walls. The dining room is a reflection of the Vermont Inn and we are now the Vermont Inn, Bill."

Bill closed his eyes, lowered his head, and then opened them, blowing out a breath of air. "Right now there are more important things we need to do to get ready for the opening. Please try to finish this as quickly as you can." He turned and walked away as Megan lifted one hand and started to respond.

Guests started arriving early on the Friday afternoon of Labor Day weekend. Megan greeted the new arrivals and Bill continued working behind the scenes, first checking a recent order of supplies from Sysco, then tallying the day's receipts and updating the budget. Megan found the rush of new guests and swirl of conversation exciting, at times stimulating, and totally exhausting. Bill seemed content to stay behind the scenes most of the time, chatting briefly with guests before excusing himself and running off to his next project. *When we pass each other in public, I get a nod and small smile. I'm starting to feel like I'm just one of the staff.*

Megan found the inn to be a demanding mistress, taking as much time as she had to give. After the last guest left on Tuesday of the long weekend, she found there was little time left for relaxing and enjoying their successful opening. *There always seems to be more to do. The only break I get is when I go outside for a walk to get a brief respite from all the work.* The telephone rang and Megan looked over as Cindy picked up the phone.

"I'm sorry you're not feeling well. Okay. Thanks for calling." Cindy looked up and made a face. Alice called in sick. She won't be in to clean rooms today."

Megan took a deep breath and smirked. "We've only been open four days. It feels more like forty days. She turned and left the lobby to get cleaning supplies for a job she didn't feel at all like doing.

Megan skipped dinner that night and sought refuge in their bedroom where she collapsed onto the bed. She lay awake, thinking about how this felt a lot like those countless times she had to prepare to entertain family or guests before they bought the inn. She'd usually do most of the de-cluttering, which meant hiding the junk out of sight, and then cleaning, vacuuming, dusting, and polishing to make the house look like it was always picture perfect: clean and casually comfortable. Then she'd have to run out to buy food and drink and think about what she'd have time to make that would be an easy prep, delicious, and with luck, an easy clean-up. If anyone happened to be staying over, that increased the amount of work. There were more rooms to clean and less places to hide the clutter, more meals to plan, and an ongoing battle to keep the house looking perfect the whole time. *Although we usually have help with some of the work here at the inn, it's a lot like having guests arrive and then leave non-stop.* She made a face. *And that's one of the less troubling things.*

Business at the inn slowed after the initial rush of opening weekend. Bill's face mirrored the financial fortunes of the inn. One of his strengths in the world of high finance was the ability to predict how political events, economic dynamics, and environmental conditions influenced stock and commodity prices. But the inn was subject to a number of factors that were far less predictable like consumer confidence and discretionary spending, weather conditions, room rate specials offered by competitors, and rising costs of attracting dependable, competent labor. He was painfully aware that by assuming a larger than anticipated mortgage, he had left himself little cushion for any downturn in business. His face told the story and Megan didn't often like what she read there.

Megan glanced over at Bill one evening after supper. He was sitting at his desk hunched over a keyboard, his face a mask of concern as he stared at figures on a spreadsheet. "Bill, can we talk about how things are going so far?"

He looked up. "Ah, sure. Let me just finish this, hon."

Megan nodded. "Okay." She went back to working on one of her relaxing activities: sudoku. She knew that her husband would be busy for a while.

She was almost finished when she heard Bill say, "What's up, Megs?"

She hesitated before answering. *Careful. Don't want to poke the bear.* "Well, I know things have been a bit slow since opening weekend. And I thought we should talk about how we're doing, financially, I mean. *Not sure I'm ready to have a conversation about how we are doing.*

He took a deep breath. "Well, I'm hoping that things pick up soon with the leaf peepers, though I've heard foliage is going to be a little later this year. We have to keep, on average, at least fifty percent occupancy in order to meet our fixed expenses." He ran his hand through his thick head of hair, a worried look crossing his face. "Right now we're doing a little worse than that, so I've been using what little cushion we have to make ends meet. We can't keep doing that much longer without making some cuts in staff and supplies."

I was afraid of this. Bill's so ready, fire, aim. We've just started and already he's worried. "We're both working overtime to make this work and I know I'm feeling a bit overwhelmed and exhausted. You must be too." She reached out and touched his arm. He looked up, clearly troubled. "I'm sure this slow patch is just temporary. I know we're heading into our busy season and will be fine once the numbers are up.

He drew his arm back. "I hope you're right, Megs." He returned to his work on the spreadsheet.

Megan was right about the numbers going up. Reservations increased to capacity at the start of foliage season at the beginning of the fourth week in September. Bill was almost cheerful when leaf peepers filled the inn. Megan had to smile when she overheard him humming a tune from a popular musical as he busily worked on payroll for staff. However, she didn't anticipate that the numbers would drop again from late October to mid-November. *The wrinkled brow again. Bill always seems to withdraw and get stressed when the numbers fall.* She walked over to him working at the computer and put an arm on his shoulder. "It'll pick up again, promise." He turned and looked up at her. "Yeah. I hope so. In my last job I used to know when these ups and downs were coming." He shook his head. "In this business it feels more like walking a tightrope, with no net to catch you if you fall." Megan nodded her head. "I hear you, love. I hear you."

Chapter 21

Bill finished looking over the Thanksgiving Day menu and hurried into the kitchen looking for their head chief. Steven was busy directing his kitchen staff on what food to prepare for dinner, the Friday before Thanksgiving. Bill stopped beside him trying but failing to wait until Steven was finished speaking. He interrupted, "Steven, do you really think we should have the Oyster Soup Appetizer as a special on our Thanksgiving Day menu?

Steven, an imposing figure in his white chef's jacket with black piping, and the inn's renowned executive chef, paused in mid-sentence and turned to Bill, considering his reply. He knew Bill was on shaky ground offering advice about things he didn't know anything about. "Well Bill, I think we need to have other choices for the patrons who might not be in the mood for a traditional dinner. Oyster Soup has always been a Christmas holiday favorite and I thought we'd give it a try. Besides, the oysters are especially fresh and tasty right now. Listen, we're pretty busy with dinner prep at the moment so maybe we could talk about this later?"

Bill hesitated a moment and frowned. He usually let Steven run the kitchen and plan the menu selections since he had been doing it long before they bought the inn. He also felt he should have more of a hand in that side of the operation. "Okay. I'd like to revisit the specials menu again before the Christmas holidays."

Steven nodded, confident he knew what was needed to run a successful restaurant. "Sure Bill. We'll talk about it before the holidays." He turned away, correcting one of the staff who was preparing a side dish with sliced brussel sprouts, pearl onions, and fresh cranberries.

Bill and Megan worked non-stop to keep up with the rush of business over the Thanksgiving weekend. It began early on Tuesday and lasted till the following Monday. It wasn't the first time since they opened the inn that they appreciated the words of the instructor at the three-day innkeeping seminar. "The art of presenting a comfortable, casual, country inn takes a lot of hard work. Your job is to make it all *look* easy—good food, great conversation, cozy accommodations, in a friendly, comfortable atmosphere."

There was another lull in the number of reservations after the Thanksgiving holidays, in part because Vermont had received very little natural snow since Thanksgiving, despite the ski slopes at Killington having their snowmaking equipment going seven days a week. Bill recalled the words of the previous owners that it really didn't matter how much snow was in Vermont. What mattered more, was how much snow there was in Boston and New York. He was worried that if their reservation numbers didn't improve, they wouldn't be able to meet their fixed expenses.

He talked again to Steven about not ordering supplies for some of the less popular items on their regular menu. Steven was surprised by the suggestion. "Bill. I've worked through the ups and downs of this business for a long time. We have regulars who come here because they like the variety of menu items. They provide a reliable income steam when other parts of the business are slow. If we start telling them some of the menu items they like are not available, we'll lose them for good.

Bill had heard this familiar argument before. "Steven, I understand how important keeping these items are to some of the regulars, but if we don't start trimming some expenses soon, we'll have to start cutting back hours or laying off staff. And I don't want to do any of those things.

Steven made a face. "Bill, the inn is already understaffed. And we're all busting our butts to make sure this place is successful."

Bill shook his head. "I just wish I had some other ideas for how we can save money. I've already dropped some of the things that make the inn a special place like having a small carafe of sherry on your dresser the day you check in, and I've hated cutting every one of them."

"I can only tell you what you need to make the dining room successful. And you're not going to do it by cutting back an already lean menu."

Bill started to respond, remembering Steven's suggestions in the past about adding more to the menu, which he opposed. Instead, he nodded at Steven and retorted, "Okay. To be continued." He left the kitchen and rounded the corner from the lounge to the sitting room. He saw Megan rearranging fruit in the bowl on the light pine coffee table. He shook his head. "Megan, we need the receipts tallied and deposited so that we can pay some bills."

Megan looked up sensing the anger and seeing the frustration etched on Bill's face. "I just finished tallying the kitchen supply orders. I was planning to do it right after lunch."

"We need it done *before* lunch" he countered, stretching out the last word.

I am getting so tired of this attitude. Megan replied, her voice rising in anger. "I'll do it after lunch. If that's not quick enough, then do it yourself."

"I *can't* do it now because I need to get office supplies for the check-in registrations this afternoon."

"I'm tired of you always telling me what to do. Receipts are usually your job. I already have a lot to do. If you need help, I told you when I could do it. As you are fond of saying, if you want it done now, then you'll have to do it yourself."

Bill's eyes got wide as the muscles in his face tensed. "Right now I have more things to do than I can handle. I need your help with some of the more critical tasks. That's the only way we can keep this place running when things get tight. Like now." Cindy, one of the inn staff, was crossing behind Bill on her way to the office. She cast a startled look at Megan and then quickly down, hurrying to leave the room.

"I'm working as hard as you are. You're just too self-centered and self-involved to notice it. And I'm not about to give up on the inn just because things get a little tight."

Bill took a breath, letting it out slowly. "Okay. Maybe I've been pushing everyone and myself too hard. And maybe that's not fair. But it's the only way I know to get too much work done by too few people."

What's happening to us? Megan wanted to keep talking about how to avoid these outbursts. *This is definitely not the best time.* She replied, letting the air out slowly between each word, "Tally the receipts. I'll do it as soon as I can get to it." Bill stared at her, looking perplexed as she turned and walked deliberately out of the room. She found Cindy working in the office.

"Cindy, I know *Bill* wants me to tally the receipts, but *I* need to go outside to calm down for a few minutes and get a little fresh air."

Cindy, a receptionist and member of the waitstaff who had worked at the inn for several years before the King's bought the inn, looked up into Megan's anxious face. "I don't blame you. Take as much time as you need. Things are good here. At least at the moment."

Megan loved to go for long walks to clear her head after completing any tedious task, like tallying the kitchen supply orders. Lately, she found a soothing peace walking through the woods, mesmerized by moving patterns of light falling on the ground's mottled leafy canvas. She struggled with nagging questions about what it took to run a successful inn and the impact it was having on her relationship with her husband. She found no easy answers in the quiet cold stillness. She suddenly stopped, staring at an unfamiliar road, startled to find herself a half mile from the inn. She turned and started back, lost in thoughts about how her life had gotten so crazy and complicated.

Chapter 22

Megan stopped, looking up at the thick dark clouds overhead, the air heavy with dampness. *Hmm, feels like snow and I'm still a good distance from the inn.* She picked up the pace.

There had always been one part of their lives that was separate, their work. Though they talked about work with each other, the likes, dislikes, hopes and fears, it was separate from their personal relationship. It never spilled over into that part of their lives. Since they bought the inn, there was no clear separation between their professional work as innkeepers and their personal relationship. They were now in business together. Partners, it was an inseparable part of who they were. They would come home now and talk about the inn, what needs to be done tomorrow, how to cut corners to save money, and nagging questions about the best way to increase their business. And most of those conversations had no easy answers. Gone was the buffer of a place to relax and just let it all go, at least for a little while. Now their relationship rose and fell with the fortunes and seasonal rhythms of the inn. When things were going well, and business was brisk but manageable, their relationship seemed to prosper, or perhaps more accurately, it didn't seem to suffer from the daily barrage of hurts and slights. But when things at the inn were going badly, and business was either terribly slow or overwhelmingly busy, their relationship was strained, difficult, and at times, frustratingly intolerable. Escape from this tension came too infrequently, and fresh hurts lingered without time or space to heal.

As Megan walked into the lobby, she stopped short. A short, heavyset woman wearing black ski pants, fur topped boots, and a lavender parka was repeatedly jabbing her finger at Cindy. "I'd like to check in now, and not wait till 3:00PM."

"Mrs. Goodman, we are still cleaning your room, but it should be ready very soon. If you'd like to have a drink at the bar, compliments of the house, I'm sure by the time you are done, it'll be ready. The woman was prepared to continue arguing when Cindy took her arm and guided her from the sitting room. "Let me show you to the lounge and get you something to drink."

Megan observed the whole episode, still standing in the doorway. *Cindy does such a good job of handling these volatile situations. Her salary will never be enough to compensate for dealing with the rude behavior of some of our guests.*

Cindy hurried back to the lobby after making the guest a vodka martini. She gave Megan a frustrated look and lowered her voice. " I had just about reached the end of my patience and was about ready to tell her to take a hike."

Megan smiled. "Cindy, you handled it perfectly. Sometimes I think telling customers to leave is the way we should treat anyone who behaves that rudely. Of course, Bill would never understand and have my head on a platter." She turned the palm of her right hand toward the ceiling and walked in a tight circle. They both laughed at the thought. Cindy returned to her work checking on reservations, her face pale in the light of the computer monitor. Her voice floated up; fingers poised over the keyboard. "I'm worried about you two." She stopped and looked up at Megan. "I worry about all the stress you guys are under and the toll it's taking on both of you."

Megan looked at Cindy a long moment before responding. "I guess I weren't really prepared for all the pressures of running an inn and it's really starting to get to us. I'm sorry you had to see that. We try hard not to let it spill over into the public side of things, but sometimes we just lose it." She turned and gazed at something unseen, far away. "I just don't have any easy answers to the never-ending demands involved in keeping this place running. I think it's turning out to be a lot more work than either one of us figured."

Cindy gave her a troubled look. "I just hope it doesn't end up with me losing my job." She lowered her voice. "They're not so easy to come by anymore."

Megan walked over and gently placed her hand on Cindy's shoulder. "The only way that would happen would be if we close the inn. And I don't see that happening anytime soon. Okay?" Cindy's reply was cut short by a weather alert.

The radio announcer sounded almost upbeat. "Snow will begin later this morning, overspreading the area from South to North. By midday, snow will increase in intensity with several inches on the ground by late afternoon. Conditions will continue to deteriorate with drifting, blowing snow and near blizzard conditions through the early evening hours. The snow will taper off before midnight with accumulations expected to be two feet or more." Cindy looked up at Megan. "Sounds like we may have some guests for an extended stay. If it gets as bad as they're saying, we'll need to do a few things now to get ready."

Megan responded with a shake of her head. "I need to pull those new quilts we bought out of storage and set them out on the beds before the guests arrive. Maybe I'll do it now before I forget."

Chapter 23

The two girls sat at a dining room table arguing about who had the nicer doll collection. Molly's face flushed as her sister ticked off her favorites. Sarah held her favorite doll in front of Molly's face, "And my most favorite is"

Suddenly, Molly grabbed her older sister's doll and ran out of the dining room, past a startled older couple, through the lobby and out of the inn. Her sister Sarah, teeth clenched, eyes fixed like twin laser beams, was two steps behind and gaining. Ted's calloused hand shot out of a row of yews along the front of the inn scooping Molly up in the air. She issued a startled scream.

"What's the hurry, little lady?"

"Let- me- go!", Molly gasped between ragged breaths.

Sarah stopped short, glaring, feet firmly planted, pointing at the doll waving wildly in Molly's hand. "She's got my doll,"

"She said her dolls were better than mine," Molly pouted.

Ted looked from Sarah to Molly. "Seems to me you both have some beautiful dolls. Let's start by giving Sarah back her doll, nicely." Molly made an unhappy face, holding out the doll to her sister while she looked away. Sarah snatched the doll and wasted no time pressing it to her chest making comforting sounds. "Good. Now, I think it's time we go in and get a little snack. How about we go into the kitchen and find some ice cream!"

"Yeah," they shouted, their anger dissolving in a burst of bright-eyed agreement. Ted left the miniature holiday lights he was stringing in a heap on the nearest shrub.

Megan watched the scene from one of the inn's front bedrooms. She smiled. *We were incredibly lucky Ted agreed to stay on when we bought the inn this summer, with a promise to stay for several more months before retiring. We never realized the enormous amount of work involved in maintaining a nineteen-room inn with a busy restaurant. And Bill is definitely not handy fixing things.*

Ted on the other hand, is the perfect handyman. He seems to revel in tackling projects of all sizes and throws himself into his work with the dedication of a religious zealot. Back in his small workshop I'm convinced he can fix anything, from old, broken wiring and lights to any kind of plumbing. He also builds and maintains things like storage and shelving to doing grounds work outside.

Megan breathed a troubled sigh leaving a moist haze on the mullioned window. *Shortly after we passed papers and the money got tight, things began to change. We began to argue about everything, even minor things became major issues. At times the tension seems almost unbearable.* Megan felt with all the building frustrations and her helplessness to do anything about it, that they were growing apart or more accurately, falling apart. To make things worse, the disagreements between them had become more heated in the last few weeks. Megan would lie awake at night trying to think of a way to avoid or at least defuse their arguments. She felt Bill had lost all reasonableness in their conversations. She would feel an uncontrollable anger whenever he questioned her about anything.

Megan looked up at the approaching gray storm clouds. *I'm glad I finally gave in to my parents repeated invitations to let the girls stay at 'Grammys' for a few days. I know how busy it can be here when it snows. I'd have so little time to watch the girls and end up feeling guilty for leaving them alone too long. And Bill loves them, but with all the pressures of this place,*

*doesn't have much time to spend with them anymore. That's
another one of those damn unknowns I was worried about.*

Molly and Sarah jumped in unison, clapping at the news
that they'd be staying at their grandparents' house in Proctor,
just a few miles away. Megan had to smile as she packed their
clothes. She knew her parents spoiled them terribly. Yet they
were really strict with her growing up. She wondered if that
was the role of grandparents, to spoil their grandchildren and
then deposit them back with their parents, leaving them to deal
with the fallout of having to say, 'no'? *Maybe it's payback for
all the trouble I caused them growing up.*

The twenty-minute trip west to Proctor gave Megan and
the girls a chance to talk about what they wanted for Christmas,
a favorite topic. As they pulled up to the old rambling Victorian
and started helping the girls with their daypacks, she could feel
the heavy cold dampness of air pregnant with the promise of
snow. She ushered the girls through the ornate front door and
heard her father approach from the dining room exclaiming,
"Who is ready for a special treat!" She just smiled and shook
her head as she greeted her Dad with a hug. After kissing the
girls goodbye, she headed out onto Route 7A South toward
Rutland. Something was bothering her, but it was just out of
reach. *I've forgotten something, but damned if I can remember
what it is.*

By the time she arrived back at the inn, snow was
already falling and had started to blanket the ground. A few
guests had checked in early, and a handful more were waiting.
She quickly threw off her coat sending a shower of flakes
across the lobby, and she began helping Cindy with
registrations. She handled with practiced patience and focused
interest the guests' endless questions about the history of the
inn, where to go for lunch, and the best conditions for skiing.
She remembered a young couple arriving late yesterday, eyes

bright with excitement and etched with a little embarrassment, joking about their lack of experience skiing, asking Megan the name of Killington's 'bunny' slope. This was a part of innkeeping that Megan really loved...the opportunity to share in animated conversation and be pulled along in the energy of their excitement. She suggested they get an early start to the slopes this morning. Killington was well known for its beginner classes that would have them up and skiing on Snowshed, their easiest slope, by lunch.

Her growling stomach reminded her that she had skipped breakfast and needed something to eat. She made her way to the kitchen and noticed a steady curtain of snow quickly piling up outside the inn. She rummaged through the cavernous Thermador refrigerator in search of cold cuts and her favorite kosher pickles. She threw together a sandwich and covered the plate with a mound of potato chips. She found an empty corner of an oversized maple cutting board and started eating the chips covering the ham and cheese sandwich. She hungrily wolfed down the food, hardly stopping to take a breath. The door from the dining room suddenly burst open, and Bill marched angrily into the room. Megan looked up, puzzled, tired, and dreading this newest outburst.

Bill stood with hands on hips, his eyes narrow slits, his mouth set in an angry scowl. "How COULD you forget?"

Megan glared at him. "What now? What did I forget?"

Bill threw up his hands. "I depend on you, Megan!"

In an exasperated tone Megan responded, "*Now* what did I do?"

Bill reached into his pocket and pulled out a stack of receipts. "It's not what you did, but what you didn't do. You forgot," he paused dramatically before continuing, "to tally these receipts." He dropped them onto the table. A look of dismay spread across Megan's face as she stared at the scattered receipts.

"Damn. I, I'm sorry. I got caught up in…"

"Megs, this was important. We needed these completed to make payroll. And it's already past bank closing hours."

Megan stood up backing away from the table, tears starting to well up. "I know, I know. I meant to do it before taking the girls to my parents' house." Her voice came out thin, ragged with emotion. She started to speak again, then looked at the disappointment etched on Bill's face. She turned, crushed by a blanket of self-rebuke and fled the kitchen, tears starting to well in the corners of her eyes. Megan walked with unseeing eyes through the busy lobby. Cindy started to speak but thought better after seeing her anguished tear-stained face. Megan grabbed her hooded anorak and rushed out of the inn and into a steady snow. Bill stormed out of the kitchen in time to see her hunched figure rush by the dining room windows, headed for the woods.

Megan marched through the intensifying storm leaving jagged scars in the deepening blanket of white. Her low-cut hiking boots and lightweight L.L. Bean jacket were no match for the relentless pounding of the driving snow. She welcomed the darkened solace of the woods, tripping over hidden tree roots lining the fast disappearing path through the forest. She kept replaying the day's events, pushing deeper into the bone-chilling forest. She almost tripped again and looked down at a set of partially filled in footprints. *Wait a minute! I must be near someone else walking in the woods.* She closed her eyes and shook her head. *God, you are so dim-witted. Those are **your** footprints!* She breathed a frustrated cloud into the snowy darkness. *Not unlike my preoccupation with the girls and getting out the quilts while missing something really important.*

She furrowed her ice-painted brow. *I'm going in circles. But for how long? It couldn't be more than 20 or 30 minutes.* Her thoughts returned to Bill. *I wonder if he's started to worry. Will he be torn between looking for me and tallying up the day's receipts?* She could almost picture him standing at the edge of the woods, a worried wrinkle playing across his forehead, rocking slightly side to side, his lips set in a grim line, his brown hair and coarse beard tinged with a frosty coating. *Will he decide that tallying the receipts is more important? Okay. That's not fair, but at the moment I feel as angry with Bill as I am at myself. Everything's a crisis to him. Everything has to be done right now. His obsession with every detail is so frustrating. And he seems to know just what buttons to push to set me off.* She took in a lungful of icy air. *I just need time to calm down and then go back. That was really stupid storming out that way, just as things were starting to get busy.* A biting gust of wind peppered her face, issuing a sharp reminder of her predicament.

Chapter 24

Megan slumped down on a log covered with freshly fallen snow. The cold and creeping fatigue conspired to sap her will to continue. A dozen thoughts competed for her attention. *The receipts! What a stupid thing to fight about. Why did I just rush out? And the inn. How did I let him talk me into buying it?* She shook her head, staring into the driving snow. *It's been nothing but a big headache. We were happy before.* She cupped her stinging hands and blew warm air into them. *I can't believe I'm wandering around in this storm. Jesus, I don't want to die out here all alone.* She involuntarily shivered. *I'm freezing my ass off.* Megan looked around at her unfamiliar surroundings, realization beginning to dawn. *It's starting to get dark, and I'm not sure where I am. I have to find my way out of here, now!*

This last panic-tinged thought seemed to galvanize her into taking action. She shook off the frosting-like coating that was rapidly covering her. *I can't stop. I have to keep going, looking for a way out.* She stumbled forward through the deepening darkness. An unseen branch scratched her face, causing her to turn away tripping into a black-green spruce branch loaded with snow. She caught the branch with both hands and immediately pushed it away shaking off the icy snow. She held her stinging hands against her cheeks for warmth. As she lifted them away, she stared at the traces of melting red-flecked snow on her fingers. *Okay, this is stupid. Stop panicking, blindly looking for a way out.* She looked around her. Nothing but darkness met her squinting gaze. *Time to start looking for shelter and get out of this fucking storm. Things must be bad. I almost never swear.*

Megan shuffled forward slowly, hands slowly waving in front of her, scanning the ground for a fallen tree or anything to use as a temporary shelter. She found a birch that had probably been knocked over during one of last summer's severe thunderstorms. It formed a narrow V with the ground resting against a small pine that kept it propped a few feet in the air. She looked around for broken branches to prop against the fallen tree. Her hands ached with the cold and she had already started to lose feeling in some of her fingers. She dragged several small limbs to the shelter, struggling to lift them high enough to prop against the fallen birch. Work was slow, and she found herself slipping and falling as she dragged the stiff, white-coated branches. She half crawled under the makeshift shelter as a wave of exhaustion swept over her. Megan pushed the snow on the ground to the edges of her sanctuary. She tucked her cold-numbed hands inside her jacket pockets and sat nestled on a bed of dead matted leaves, her head just inches from fragrant pine branches overhead. She desperately tried to think of where the inn might be from here and how she might find her way out but found it difficult to resist a seductive desire to drift into a deep peaceful sleep.

A pine branch high above, overloaded with freshly fallen snow issued a sharp, resounding crack. It fell, landing on her crudely constructed shelter. Megan startled awake, momentarily disoriented. *Where the hell am I?. Oh yeah, shit.* Fortunately, the broken limbs covering her protected lair absorbed most of the weight of the fallen branch. She painfully inched herself out of her makeshift sanctuary, got up stamping in small circles and angrily shook her head. Panic had started to claw at her stomach. *No. Not going to die here.* Her eyes narrowed, her mouth set in a grim line, her face a steely mask. *Use your head, stupid.* She took a deep breath, stopped and looked around her, seeing nothing in the swirling white darkness. She walked in small circles, surprised not to feel any branches. *I'm in the middle of a small clearing in the woods. Odd.* She explored the edges of the open space, hoping to find another place to seek shelter, by feeling the tips of tree branches and moving to her right, navigating the uneven edges of the clearing.

Before she had gone halfway around, she found she was only a feet away from a shadow that was definitely not a tree. It puzzled her at first, and then made her straighten up and exclaim, "It looks like a kid's playhouse!" She edged closer to the dark outline. It was a complete miniature one-room playhouse with a half-height door and two real windows. She couldn't remember seeing one in the woods before. She knew it couldn't be more than a few hundred or so yards from the edge of someone's property. *Maybe I should march right out of the woods back to the nearest house for help.* She looked around and realized she didn't have a clue which direction to go. *There's nothing that looks familiar in this darkness. Well, if I do decide to stay here, I better make sure it's in one piece.* She slowly shuffled around the perimeter, tapping her hand on the sides of the playhouse. It seemed to be paneled with horizontal pieces of clapboard siding. The walls still looked solid as did the shingled roof, covered with a layer of dead pine needles and topped with a frosting of snow. She carefully made her way back around to the front of the playhouse and found the door. She knelt in the snow. *There's no door knob, just a simple handle.* She gave it a push and the door sprung open. *Must be just a simple door catch keeping it closed.* She crawled inside and turned and tried closing the door. It took a number of tries to push the drifted snow that filled the doorway back outside. On her final push, she heard the door catch make a satisfying click. She felt something brush by her fingers. *Feels like a swinging door latch. Clever kids. I'll bet they added that to keep out unwanted visitors.* She set the door latch into the wooden holder.

The inside was cold, quiet and amazingly airtight. Megan moved around on her knees, carefully feeling her way around the inky-black interior. She bumped into two small straight-backed chairs on either side of a tiny table. In a corner, she found a dented cabinet that looked like it had been discarded during a kitchen renovation. She held her breath as she grasped the smooth round knob handles and opened the doors. She felt inside. To her surprise on the top shelf, was a collection of different candles and matches. *Kids, your parents might be angry about having these matches, but I'm so happy you do!* She removed the largest candle in a glass jar that was missing a cover. It had a chiclet-sized chip of glass missing from its rim. She fumbled with the matches trying to light the wick. Her fingers were so stiff, she dropped the first match into the jar. *Okay, I can do this. Just take it slow.* She carefully held the second match and awkwardly struck the flint several times, finally managing to coax a spark into life. She held the small flame against the wick, watching it catch, then blossom into a bright glow, sending a warm light through the playhouse.

Megan cupped her hands over the bouncing flame trying to feel her frozen fingers. She continued her explorations holding the candle up close to the cabinet shelves. On the second shelf, she discovered a small tin. Inside it were two unopened chocolate chip granola bars and three gummy bears that all appeared to be unmolested. On the bottom shelf was an assortment of old baseball hats, a small pocket knife, a curved plastic pirate sword, a comic book, and a billy club. Megan took out two wool sweaters that looked decidedly homemade, explaining why they found their way out of the public eye and into the playhouse. She decided she'd use them to sit or sleep on later. On the other side of the playhouse, she found a four-foot bench that was narrow, but long enough to sleep on if she curled up. She also discovered a shelf under one of the windows with an assortment of chipped mugs and plastic plates, a small pot and a warming stand with votive candles for keeping the contents warm. *Maybe it'll be okay if I can wait here until the storm is over. I think I'll heat some water. And do I dare try to eat one of the granola bars? Fuck it!* Her fingers were too stiff to unwrap the bar, so she used her teeth to rip it open. She took a sizeable bite, having to pry a frozen chunk off with her molars. *God, how could something so old taste so good?* She was tempted to eat more, but knew she shouldn't use up all of her precious supplies. She grabbed one of the pots and walked over to the door. Bracing her weight against it, she undid the latch and slowly pulled it open enough to reach through the opening and packed the pot full of snow. She shivered as she struggled to close the door and reset the latch. *What I won't do to make a fancy meal.* She lit two of the votive candles and placed the small pot on top of the stand.

She stomped around in the flickering light of the playhouse waiting for the snow to melt, then get warm. When steam started rising from the pot, she poured the water into one of the chipped mugs. *It'll never get hot, but warm feels wonderful right now.* She held the mug for a moment, savoring the warmth on the inside of her hands and the faint trace of steam rippling over her lashes and ice coated hair. She slowly sipped the clear liquid. She took one of the smaller candles to the single-paned window, lit it, placed it on a chipped plate and slid it on to the sill. She took a second one, lit it, put it on a pickle jar cover, then placed it on the ledge of the other window. She made lumpy cushions out of the old sweaters and curled up on the bench. *I wonder if this warmth I'm starting to feel is from the candles, the tea, or just a very old memory of a poor little match girl.*

She closed her eyes and conjured up images of a flickering fireplace and a bottle of rich, fragrant red wine as she stretched out on a deeply cushioned leather sofa. In the background, she imagined Bill scurrying around like a bushy haired brown rat, checking to make sure all of the windows were locked. He was mumbling over and over, *If I want it done right, I'll have to do it myself.* She could only manage to shiver in her drowsy stupor at the fanciful images.

Megan awoke with a start. The small candles she had placed on the sills had gone out. She started to scold herself when she stopped, cocking her head to one side. *What the hell is that? That faint scratching sound? Gone. Must be my imagination. Oh shit, it's back. And more insistent. Maybe it's just the tree branches. Strange. It starts, gets louder, then suddenly stops. There it is again.* She began to stand but found she had to stoop slightly. Her stiff leg muscles shrieked in protest. She went to the window, trying to see what might be making the sound, but the snow and darkness conspired to block her view. *Yeah, I could open the door and check outside. I've seen horror movies with scenes like that. I'd be screaming at the screen. No. Don't be an idiot! DO NOT OPEN the door!* She smiled grimly. *Well, I suppose there's always that possibility, but I do know once I open it, I probably won't be able to close it again.* She looked around in the darkness. *I need to find something in here to use as a weapon to ward off any unwelcome guests, just in case.* She remembered the billy club and felt her way to the cabinet to retrieve it.

She returned to her makeshift bed, hoping to return to her pleasant dream of wine and a warm fireplace. She turned and moved several times, trying to find a comfortable position. There was a soft muffled tap. *Okay. That's different.* She looked over at one of the windows. A pair of small yellow eyes appeared briefly, scanning the interior, then vanished. She sat bolt upright, tightly clutching the wooden club. *Shit! This is no horror movie and there's only room for one of us in here, whatever you are.* It took several minutes for the violent pounding in her chest to subside. Megan settled back on the bench, holding the club close. She felt herself drifting to a dark twisted place filled with silent roaming yellow-eyed shadows.

Chapter 25

Heidi and Dave had come to Vermont early in the winter season to ski the big mountain as Killington was affectionately called. They had heard about the Vermont Inn and its exceptional food from a close friend who had died in a car accident the previous summer. It was partly in tribute to his memory that the couple came to the inn. They listened to the weather report early in the morning and decided that the forecast for heavy snow due later in the day wouldn't stop their first experience using downhill skis. Light snow hadn't yet started when they left the inn for the slopes after breakfast.

She smiled staring out the side window as the trees rushed by in a blur, thinking about the first time she met Dave. Heidi had always loved the outdoors. She bumped into Dave while staying at an AMC Lodge at the base of Mount Washington as part of a hiking weekend with friends in the White Mountains. The first evening in the large main dining hall she tripped on the leg of Dave's chair and accidentally dropped her tray of food on him. His startled reaction quickly gave way to good-natured teasing.

"So, do you always make new friends by dropping chili and apple cobbler on them?"

Heidi laughed, clearly embarrassed. "No. I save that for my special new friends." She held out her hand. "Hi. I'm Heidi."

He couldn't help but smile back. "Hi. It's Dave."

She knelt down trying to help clean up the mess. "And I hope you'll consider joining me and my friends tomorrow. We're hiking up Mt. Washington."

Dave looked surprised. "Well, I accept on one condition. That you promise not to drop any more of your food on me."

Heidi stood up and held up one hand, a mock serious look on her face. "Dave, I solemnly promise to do my best not to drop anymore food on you, today."

He laughed replying, "A statute of limitations. Aren't you the clever girl. I guess we have a deal."

Dave seemed to have a way of making Heidi feel at ease, even in awkward situations. The next day's hike was all the more enjoyable with Dave's easy-going banter and mischievous sense of humor. The weekend ended with promises to get together again soon. It wasn't long before they were spending all of their weekends together.

They hurried under the Killington arch to the cashier booth and paid for two - one-day 'learn and ski' packages. By the time Dave was fitted for his boots and skis, he could feel the sweat start to trickle under his arms. They walked awkwardly in their coffin-like ski boots toward the practice slopes casting nervous glances at each other while awkwardly trying to cradle their skis and poles. Heidi laughed at Dave when he turned to look back at the lodge and almost knocked her over with his skis.

He started to apologize, but she interrupted saying, "You know what they say about payback."

"I've seen what you're capable of and that's what has me worried."

Most of the morning was spent following the patient directions of the ski instructor as they practiced stopping, starting, and snowplow turns. During one attempt to stop, Heidi reached out, poles waving in the air, and managed to topple Dave who made the mistake of being too close to her. They both went down in a tangle of skis and poles, laughing until their sides hurt. After a quick lunch in the damp, noisy snow loft cafeteria, they were ready to try Snowshed, one of the easiest trails on the mountain, on their own.

They spent more time laughing then actually skiing at each other's spills and awkward attempts to get up again. More than once, Heidi would scoop up a handful of snow and hurl it at Dave. The first time he laughed and said, "I guess our chili deal doesn't cover snow!" He then gathered up an armful of snow and dumped it on her head. By late afternoon they were thoroughly wet, tired, sore and ready to leave. The snow had changed from light flurries to a driving wall of white, quickly burying the buildings at the base of the mountain under a heavy blanket. They returned their rented skis, poles, and boots and intended to leave for the inn. However, they couldn't resist stopping to rest in front of the roaring fire at the base lodge, watching the steam lazily rise from their still wet entwined fingers. They looked at each other and decided to celebrate making it through their first skiing adventure alive and in one piece. They opted to indulge with one of their favorite drinks…a nutty Irishman. This heart-warming concoction of hot coffee, Bailey's Irish Crème, Frangelico, topped with whipped cream and a dash of cinnamon, gently warmed them inside as their parka's dried near the fire. They sipped slowly, savoring the sweet nutty coffee flavor and relishing their comfortable drowsy stupor. As Dave finished his drink, he looked over and noticed Heidi starting to nod off.

He reached over and gave her arm a gentle nudge. "Okay, sleepyhead. I think we better head back before we both fall asleep."

Reluctantly they pulled back on their boots, hats, gloves, and warmed parka's, bracing for the deteriorating weather conditions outside. Their legs felt leaden as they held onto each other and trudged through the fast accumulating snow toward their white-capped car. Heidi stopped suddenly and pulled Dave close. She stood on tiptoe and kissed him gently on the lips. "You. You make everything, even the first time on skis, fun."

Dave took a breath, letting the moist air slowly escape, enveloping her face in a tender cloud. He held her gaze for a long moment. "Everything I say feels like a tired cliché. But my heart is so full of love, I can't imagine my life without you." He looked down at his ungloved hand, then started speaking in a creepy voice. "My fingers have turned into small icicles that long to stroke your pretty face." He slowly lifted his arm toward her, his eyes wide, an evil mischievous grin spreading across his face.

She intercepted his fingers. "Oh, no you don't mister snow monster! You need to warm up those icicles before any touching happens."

"Well, in that case I suggest we continue this conversation someplace warmer...like the car."

"And somewhere more private," she responded raising one eyebrow.

"Yes, indeed, my little snow bunny."

As they reached the car, Dave exclaimed, "I can't believe how much snow there is already!" He reached across and arm-brushed the several inches off the windshield. He jumped into the driver's seat, started the car, and they both sat waiting for the engine to warm up. They held each other's hands as they watched the wipers beat a rhythm across the windshield.

"If I don't start for the inn soon, I think morning will find us buried here. I just need to brush the snow from the rest of the windows."

"Well, I'm glad you're doing it. I don't think I have enough energy to lift my arms. I'm totally exhausted and everything I have on is still damp."

"I hope not totally exhausted." Dave replied with a mischievous smile."

Heidi rolled her eyes and motioned with her head toward the door. "Well in that case, you energizer bunny, I guess you better get brushing."

Dave eased the Ford Taurus out of the parking lot and up the hill to the Killington access road. He struggled to keep the fishtailing car on the road as massive plows fought a losing battle to keep the highway clear. Traffic on Route 4 had already slowed to a crawl as two-wheel drive cars struggled to negotiate the massive string of mountains. The ten-minute ride slowed to almost forty. Dave turned the car off the highway sliding sideways up the short access road to the inn. As he pulled into an empty space opposite the front of the inn, he felt a wave of exhaustion wash over him. He reached over and took Heidi's hand. "I don't know about you, but my legs feel like rubber. How about we hit the hot tub?"

Heidi laughed. "If I'm able to climb in, I might not be able to climb out." She looked over at Dave and smiled. "But what a great way to go."

They found it slow going trying to unzip and unbutton their damp, sweaty ski clothes. Heidi looked up as she fumbled with a button on the side of her ski pants. "Even my fingers are too tired to work."

Dave laughed. "Keep telling them, hot tub, hot tub, hot tub."

They pulled on swimsuits and bathrobes, then walked the narrow corridor following it downstairs to the hot tub/exercise room. They threw off their robes and gingerly slid into the steaming bubbly water. Dave, a psychologist with a private practice, chatted about how he loved watching people interact with one another, interpreting their actions through facial expressions, and pondering the possible causes of their behavior. Heidi raised her eyebrows remarking, "Well, doctor, I'll be sure and take care what I say and do around you." Dave feigned hurt, splashing water on Heidi, causing her to squeal with laughter and retaliate, which escalated into a full-scale noisy water battle. They stopped, both out of breath from laughing.

Dave held up a hand and called a truce. "And every truce demands the parties shake hands or…," Dave pulled Heidi, close wrapping his arms around her, "engage in a passionate, soul-sucking kiss."

Heidi screamed in laughter, pushing him away and splashing water on him. "Get away from me you nasty, evil, dementor." At that moment, the pulsing aerated water stopped as the soft lighting inside the hot tub went out. The emergency lights above the entrance came on momentarily before the regular lighting returned. She looked around the room. "Jesus. Now I think you really must be a dementor!"

Dave gave Heidi an evil smile, raising both hands out of the hot tub and into the air. "I have limitless powers and now you are mine." Heidi laughed and splashed more water on him. He wiped the water out of his eyes as the lights started to flicker again. "It looks like the storm is playing havoc with the power. I think we need to continue my attempts at soul sucking back in the room."

Heidi stood up slowly, steam rising as water dripped from her body. "I know I'm cooked." She grimaced as she lifted her legs over the side of the tub, grabbing a towel and wrapping it around her. "God, I feel like a million years old." She pushed her hair away from her face and looked back at Dave. He was smiling as he watched her. "And I'll have no nasty comments from the dementor gallery."

Chapter 26

Bill nodded at the happy couple in bathing suits and towels as they squeezed past him on the second-floor corridor laughing playfully. *Megan has been gone now for over an hour, and it's already dark outside. How far could she have gone on foot in this weather? She should be back by now.* He walked downstairs and looked around the lounge, hoping to see her interacting with the guests. *Damn.*

The lounge was a small comfortable refuge between the lobby and dining room. The bar itself was ten feet long, made from a thick slab of Vermont cherry that would seat four or five adults. In back of the bar sat a modest collection of liquors on two shelves, as well as an assortment of domestic and imported beer and wines. A cable TV sat perched on the wall at one end of the bar. At the moment, there were a few customers sitting at the bar staring into their drinks and a few chatting at some of the tables. Most of the customers were young, probably skiers looking to get away from a winter-weary city for a long weekend. Bill floated among the guests reassuring them that this storm would be a memorable part of their trip. *This is what Megan does so well.* He kept glancing out of the window, hoping the snow drumming against the windows would subside soon and they'd be off of the backup generators. Cindy was busy filling orders and helping the bartender with the easier drinks. She noticed that Bill spent much of his time preoccupied with the storm outside. She felt sure it had something to do with Megan, who she hadn't seen since late afternoon.

The TV interrupted a rerun of the Simpsons with a winter weather advisory for Central Vermont. The room grew silent as a serious meteorologist pointed to a powerful northeaster sweeping up the coast. He pointed to the map, showing the worst conditions would be in western Massachusetts, west and central New Hampshire, all of Vermont, and the easternmost part of central and northern New York. He ended, predicting continued heavy snowfall with blizzard-like conditions through early evening with expected accumulations in the mountains of over three feet. Bill listened with his mouth partly open, his eyes glued to the screen. As the television returned to the Simpsons, Bill turned and walked to one of the windows, staring anxiously at the swirling storm outside.

Normally, Cindy avoided asking Bill questions about what was going on and felt more comfortable talking to Megan. She decided, however, that this just seemed too important to leave alone and, the guests were starting to sneak looks over at his apprehensive face staring out the window. She made her way over to him and lightly touched his arm. He jumped, startled at the intrusion into his troubled thoughts. "Jesus! You startled me!"

"Sorry." She took a step back and whispered, "What's wrong, Bill?", above the buzz of conversation in the bar.

Bill hesitated, debating what to tell her. "I'm worried about Megan. She went for a walk more than an hour ago and still hasn't returned," he replied, turning to face her.

"Yeah, I saw her leave. I'm sure she probably stopped at Nancy's place and is waiting for the storm to let up."

He shook his head. "I know she would have called by now. Besides, I saw her heading towards the woods on the other side of the pool."

"Why don't we get some help to look for her? If she's found quickly, the worst thing that will happen will be she'll feel a little embarrassed."

It's true. I'd rather have Megan safe back here and angry with me for making a fuss than out in this storm. Why is this so hard for me to admit? He took a deep breath, seeming to make up his mind. "Thanks Cindy. I know you are probably right. I'll contact Sergeant Greene at the station." He turned and hurried into the receptionist's office off the sitting room. He punched in the number of the Rutland police and asked for the Sergeant.

After a long pause, Greene's voice boomed through the earpiece. "Sergeant Greene, may I help you?"

"Hi Spencer, Bill King."

"Hi, Bill. All this snow should be good for business. What can I do for you?"

"It's Megan. She went out for a walk over an hour ago and hasn't returned. It isn't like her to stay out like this during the busiest time of the day, and I'm worried something's wrong."

"Have you checked to see that she hasn't just stopped at someone's house waiting for the storm to pass?"

"I saw her head into the woods on the path in front of the pool. There's nobody for a good distance near there, and I know she would have called me if she stopped somewhere."

"Hmmm. Well, I can put out word for our patrols to keep an eye out along Route 4 and the side roads. But the conditions are deteriorating, and it would be dangerous to do any searching right now. And with this power outage, we're just trying to keep up with emergency calls. I'm hearing from new parents who are concerned about their newborn babies to elderly folks who have lost heat and worried about freezing to death."

"I know you have your hands full. I just don't know what else to do short of going out looking for Megan myself."

"That would be a mistake, Bill. Then there would be two of you lost in the woods and in trouble."

"I know. I know. Don't worry. I'm not going to do anything stupid. I'll wait until I hear from you or the storm lets up, and I can set out on one of our snowmobiles."

"I'll send a car up there as soon as I can, to look around and see if we can help locate her, okay?"

"Thanks, I'll let you know if she shows up at the inn."

"Let's hope so."

Bill turned from the phone and stared absentmindedly at the large wall calendar with important events scribbled in Megan's handwriting. He knew the police would have increasing difficulty finding Megan during the next few hours if she really was lost. Momentarily he considered disregarding his promise to Spencer and heading out on one of their two snowmobiles. He knew that darkness and decreasing visibility in the storm would make that choice both dangerous and foolhardy.

Part 3: Deadly Pursuit

Chapter 27

Lou Vitelli had switched to the left lane, pulling even with the bus, hoping Benny would see his flashy car and panic. He kept trying to look up at the windows. "I'll bet that little rat is shitting in his drawers right about now. We'll get him when the bus makes that stop in Lebanon." The car in front of him pulled in front of the bus and Vitelli found himself looking at the back of a sander truck. He grimaced as he heard the sand-salt mixture peppering the front of his car. "Fuck, that shit's going to ruin the finish." His mouth turned into a frustrated scowl as he slowed, watching the bus move several car lengths ahead. He moved into the middle lane and saw the bus's right turn signal flash as it moved into the right lane.

Vitelli turned to Rocco. "I'm not worried. Benny's not getting away from this little baby." He patted the dashboard. Rocco cast a nervous glance at his boss's determined expression. Vitelli had missed the snow crusted sign for Route 89 North, not expecting the off-ramp to come up so soon. He saw the brake lights on the bus briefly appear as it slowed, then disappear as it turned onto the off-ramp.

***

Benny woke with a start as the bus's air brakes snapped his head forward and back. As the Greyhound slowed and turned onto the off ramp from Route 93 to Route 89, it started a slow uncontrolled slide toward the guard rail. Years of experience had taught the driver to resist jamming on the brakes and instead apply steady pressure, coaxing the wheels gently to change direction. There was a collective gasp from the passengers, followed by a nervous low buzz of conversation. As the brakes started to gain traction, the bus slowed, then almost imperceptibly began to change direction. With agonizing slowness, it headed back toward the middle of the icy off ramp, just inches from the guard rail. It emerged at a crawl onto Route 89. John took a deep breath, then picked up his cabin mic. "I am really sorry about that scare folks. As you can see, the weather conditions are deteriorating, and the roads are getting more slippery. I'll be reducing our speed to make sure we travel the rest of the way safely." Benny heard disgruntled rumblings, but no further outburst from Mr. Finch.

***

Vitelli needed to move to the right lane to make the exit ramp. "Oh crap!" He looked quickly to his right. There was a car next to him. He licked his lip and hit the gas, moving dangerously close to the car in front of him. He wrenched the wheel to the right to change lanes. The nose of the car turned slightly to the right, but it kept traveling straight. In desperation, Vitelli began to pump the brakes. The vehicle slowed as the brakes gained traction and it skidded sideways into the right lane. The car behind leaned on its horn. "Shut the fuck up, asshole!" His car was fast approaching the off-ramp to Route 89. "I can't miss this exit! I'll never catch him."

Vitelli had momentarily straightened the wheels but now was almost opposite the off ramp. He turned the wheel hard to the right, hitting the brakes. The nose of the car still headed straight but slid sideways off the highway and onto the off-ramp. The car lightly bounced off the guard rail, turning it sideways, metal scraping, screeching in protest.

Wild-eyed and disbelieving, Vitelli screamed, "Fuck, fuck, fuck!" The Porsche barely slowed sliding down the ramp until it reached a bank of snow piled against the guard rail at the bottom of the ramp curve. Rocco sat white-faced, fingernails digging into the seat bottom, mouth drawn tight, eyes frozen open in terror. The car rode up the snow bank and momentum lifted it over the guard rail. Rocco heard Vitelli howl, "SHIT", immediately before the car slammed down on its side, the driver's window exploding inside the car. The crippled cherry red Porsche slid nose first down the embankment before it smashed into a stand of maple trees at the bottom of the steep incline. It hesitated a moment, peppered with clumps of snow shaken from the trees, then rolled slowly, metal groaning in protest, landing right-side-up with a dull thump, the red hood partially buried in deep snow.

Rocco sat dazed and disorientated, but miraculously unhurt except for an egg-sized bump on top of his head. He looked over at Vitelli who was slumped deathly still, the side of his tanned face resting against the steering wheel, his head turned toward him looking out with empty eyes. Blood streamed from multiple head wounds like thin red fingers raking down across his face and dripping silently onto his wool pants.

Rocco struggled to open the door, pushing against it with his elbow. In frustration he leaned back and threw his shoulder against it. The door burst open. He struggled to release his seat belt, then rolled out of the seat into a bed of icy white. His head was immediately buried in snow as his knees and legs sank out of sight. He lifted his face and shook off the frosty coating. He rolled onto his side, then rocked back and forth a number of times trying to sit up, before finally succeeding. He shook his head, watching his moist breath billow out around him in a cloud.

Fuck me. I am so done with all this shit. Rocco turned, squinting as he looked up the incline into the blinding curtains of snow. He could barely discern outlines of people fifty feet above him. One had a flashlight, a tiny waving pinprick of light. He weakly raised his arm and started to wave, wondering how anyone could possibly see him, sitting hunched over half buried in the snow.

Chapter 28

Nia leaned forward on her desk chair, her fingers stabbing a few keys. She stopped, staring at the first few words on the screen and sat back, her mind miles away. *Sometimes it feels like everything I touch leaves. No, more like flees in terror or worse, dies.* She looked away from the screen at the picture of her standing in front of her Dad in uniform. They were both smiling broadly. He had both arms crossed in front of her. *I don't remember when that was taken. Couldn't have been more than ten.* Nia took a deep breath. *Knew that's what I always wanted to do.*

A booming voice from behind startled her. "How's that report coming, Detective D'Amato?"

She turned and looked at the gray-haired, barrel-chested Deputy Commander. "Sir, I was just starting to write it up. I'll have it on your desk before the end of the day." He nodded and walked away. Nia was one of the newer detectives in the department, although she had already been there over seven years. *I keep thinking that must be the reason why he's still looking over my shoulder. Maybe I'm just being overly sensitive. Yeah, no. I should know better.* Nia had more than once considered asking him to back off and let her do her job. But she envisioned the outcome being a confrontation with an exchange of heated words. *And that would lead to a charge of insubordination, and suspension without pay. Just what I need to get ahead in the Department.* She stared at her humorless smile reflected in the monitor, her fingers still poised over the keys. *Maybe it's not about getting ahead.*

She looked up. *Shit. It's after five o'clock. Time to finish this thing and get the hell out of here.* Thirty minutes later Nia read over her report with the mouse poised over the send button. She made a face. *I always did suck at spelling.* She hit a few keys, corrected two errors, then sent the report off to the Deputy Commissioner. *There you go. Are you satisfied now? Will you ever be satisfied?*

Nia leaned back in her chair. *Inertia's a bitch. I just need the energy to get up and go.* She reviewed the few details she knew about the victim. *Caulder was a loner. Didn't have a social life. His limp would be a liability, socially as well as physically. Probably had trouble making friends. When he was younger, he would have been teased unmercifully. Probably considered the jewels as a ticket out of his unhappy life and a chance to start again. It begins to make sense why he went to a pawn shop. But two million in retail value diamonds would be way out of Bobby's league. I wonder if the slime ball blew him off or referred him to one of his contacts? One of them did lie about looking at a Seiko watch. Bobby wouldn't have any reason to lie. But, Caulder was nervous and obviously second-guessing what Bobby might say.*

If I confront Bobby, he'll stick to his story and won't be intimidated into giving me any names. Best-case scenario is he would lie and say he refused to have anything to do with any stolen diamonds. I know that somehow Caulder got connected with a fence to sell the diamonds for a price. And it looks like that fence double-crossed him and decided to keep the money and steal the stones. Caulder had planned to leave the city by bus, probably as soon as he could. His killer would have had plans to leave town after the double cross as well. Probably wouldn't have been by bus. I'd guess it would have been by car or train since the airport had closed in the storm. I wonder if finding the bus ticket caused him to change his mind? Or was it something else?

Nia's phone rang. It was Deputy Commander Flynn. "Detective D'Amato. We just got word from the State Police in Manchester, New Hampshire that Lou Vitelli was killed in an accident on an off-ramp to Route 89 North. His passenger, Rocco Fucillo, escaped serious injury in the crash. Rocco refuses to answer any questions about where they were going in the middle of a snowstorm, but I thought it might be connected to your suspect possibly leaving town by bus."

"Thank you, Deputy Commander. I'll follow-up on that." The line clicked off.

Nia looked up, following the cracks in the plaster. *So, the perp might have been connected to Lou Vitelli. And he would have been carrying a large amount of money. Was it money belonging to Vitelli? Did the perp do a runner and Vitelli decide to chase after him? It seems unlikely that a crime boss would be crazy enough to do that. But there had to be a lot of money involved, given the number of diamonds. Probably over six figures. That's a lot of incentive for someone to steal the money and for Vitelli to head out into a snowstorm.* She reached for the phone and dialed a contact in vice. "I need to check for known associates of Vitelli who might broker a six-figure diamond deal."

Fifteen minutes later, Nia had a list of eight names. She knew any of them could have met with Will Caulder. And at least half of them matched the description of the obnoxious passenger. She shook her head. *I know. He might not even be our perp. And it might not make any difference. That bus will be crossing the border in a couple of hours.*

Chapter 29

The Greyhound crawled up Route 89 slower than its usual 65 miles per hour, buffeted by occasional gusts of wind and a thin icy screen of snow. The bus driver had to constantly monitor the position of the bus as it slid on drifts of wind-blown snow hiding an icy layer beneath. It came dangerously close to cars attempting to pass on his left on more than one occasion. His radio crackled to life with a bulletin from the New Hampshire State police. "Be advised that we have closed the ramp from Route 93 North to Route 89 North. A car has skidded off the road and there is a report of a possible fatality." John struggled to see through the snowy streaks on the windshield. *I guess we dodged a bullet on that one. If we had left any later, we'd still be sitting in traffic waiting to get off of 93.* John picked up the cabin mic. "I'm sorry for the interruption, folks. Given our reduced travel speed due to the deteriorating road conditions, I'm not going to make our usual ten-minute stop at the mall in Lebanon, NH.

The only response was a barely audible, "Thank God for small favors," from a familiar voice in the darkened back of the bus.

After 45 minutes of worsening conditions, the radio next to John crackled to life. "This is a special traffic bulletin from the Vermont State Police. We are closing Route 89 north of Hanover, New Hampshire, just over the state line in Vermont. This is due to a gasoline truck that has jack-knifed across all lanes. Fuel is spilling out onto the roadway. It will take several hours for us to contain the spill and clean up all the fuel. Please stay tuned to this frequency for updates."

John took a deep breath and picked up the mic. "Sorry again for the interruption folks, but I'll need to take an alternate route to Montreal because the road is closed up ahead due to a bad accident on Route 89 just over the state line."

A few chuckles greeted Finch's comment, "God, we're never going to get to Canada on dead hound, the slowest bus company in the fucking world." John could only smile and shake his head.

He turned off of Interstate 89 and headed west toward Rutland, Vermont. John intended to follow U.S. Route 4 west across central Vermont to Route 7 and then turn north toward Montreal. After an hour of fighting the intensifying storm, he slowed to a crawl as he approached two banks of flashing blue lights ahead. A state trooper approached the driver's window. John pushed it open and was greeted with a blast of stinging snow.

A voice boomed from deep inside a dark blue parka. "Evening sir. A major power line has just come down east of Rutland. It's blocking Route 4 westbound and eastbound. We've been told because of the storm it will take several hours to clear the road and repair the damage. All traffic around Rutland is being diverted. You can either turn around or seek temporary shelter at one of the places east of Rutland that has backup power."

John thanked the trooper and eased the bus away from the flashing lights. *Turning around is not an option.* He remembered an inn his family visited once several years ago nestled at the bottom of one of the Green Mountains, just off Route 4. It had a cozy sitting room and fireplace, a lounge with a well-stocked bar and a well-known restaurant. He knew it might be a long shot, but it would beat sitting on the bus for three or four hours with his obnoxious passenger, waiting for the roads to clear. He hoped the inn would be one of those having power and would be able to accommodate everyone so the passengers could get something to eat and drink.

He reluctantly picked up the microphone. "I'm sorry to keep bothering you with these announcements. I've just learned from the state police that they have had to close the road on Route 4 near Rutland due to downed power lines across the road. I think the safest thing we can do is get off the road while we wait for them to make repairs and open the road again. I'm planning to stop at an inn a little further ahead on Route 4 and see if they might be able to accommodate those of you who would like drinks and maybe dinner." He heard Finch grumble as he made the announcement, then loudly broadcast his complaints as soon as he finished. He leapt from his seat and stomped to the front of the bus, stopping immediately behind the driver.

"What do you mean you're stopping? We can't stop. This bus is *supposed* to be a non-stop to Montreal"

John responded with growing frustration. "Mr. Finch. Perhaps you misunderstood my announcement. The road ahead has been *shut down*."

"Why don't we take a different route to Montreal? We couldn't be more than a couple of hours away."

"If we get off on some back-country road in these conditions, we'll most likely get stuck. Then we'll be sitting for many hours waiting for a heavy-duty tow truck to pull us out. If we are lucky enough *not* to get stuck, the lowered speeds on country back roads and added miles would ensure we wouldn't get there much before morning. However, if we just *wait* a few hours until the power lines are repaired, we can continue onto Route 7, then back onto Route 89 all the way to Montreal."

With eyes flashing, Finch spun in place and in a high grating voice exclaimed to everyone on the bus, "Well *I* don't *like* your plan! You seem to be doing your best to avoid getting us to Montreal."

"Mr. Finch, please sit down." *Finch. Again. I'm tempted to add, before I throw you off this bus.* The driver had been trying to give Mr. Finch a wide berth. *He's one of the angriest, rudest customers I've experienced in a long time.*

It took the Greyhound another thirty minutes to reach the inn. John slowly turned the bus off Route 4 onto Cream Hill Road, plowing through a soft arc of drifting snow. A hundred yards up the road he turned right into the parking lot of the Vermont Inn. He was encouraged to see that the trees on either side of the entrance sparkled with soft circles of miniature white lights coated with newly fallen snow. The bus full of restless passengers slid to a stop outside the door of the inn. John turned in his seat. "Folks, I know *most* of you have been very patient." He looked at the sour face on Mr. Finch. "Please wait here until I have a chance to talk to the owners about whether they can accommodate us."

An angry voice from the middle of the bus erupted. "And how long are we going to be here at this *unscheduled* stop?"

John turned, looking daggers at his disruptive passenger. "Mr. Finch. I assure you; it won't be any longer than necessary. Believe me, I want to get to Montreal as much as you do." He heard a disgruntled snort as he turned and left the bus. *No, make that a hell of a lot more than you do, Mr. Finch.*

Chapter 30

As John stepped off the bus, he took a step, lost his footing and fell hard on the slippery snow-covered pavement. He shook his head as he brushed the snow off his uniform, hoping his fall went unobserved. He turned and walked gingerly across the parking lot, under the green canopy and through the heavy wooden door. He entered the lobby and saw no one at the registration counter. There were a few folks lounging in the sitting room to his left, and a low buzz of conversation coming from the bar to his right. He turned and walked into the bar, nearly colliding with Bill who was headed to retrieve the dinner reservation list.

"Whoa, excuse me!" exclaimed Bill. "Can I help you, sir?"

The driver stopped short, looking up. "Yes, you can. I nearly killed myself walking up to the front entrance. And I'm looking for the owner."

"I am. Sorry about that. We have been trying to stay ahead of all this snow and keep the parking lot clear, but I'm afraid it's a losing battle." He stuck out his hand. Hi, I'm Bill King, the owner. My wife Megan and I run the Vermont Inn."

The driver seemed taken aback for a moment, but quickly recovered. He reached out and shook the offered hand. "Hi, I'm John Doherty, a driver for Fleet Greyhound and we're headed to Montreal. I've got a busload of hungry and thirsty passengers, and it looks like we're not going much further in this storm with the power lines down. We'd like to stop here for food and drinks, if you think you'll be able to handle the crowd."

Bill hesitated, a troubled look crossing his face. *How can I take on this added work, with Megan still missing and the police on their way to start looking for her? A busload of passengers will place a tremendous burden on our already reduced staff.* "Well, I need to check and see if we can handle the added customers and make sure we have room."

John interrupted, holding up a hand. "Look, if this is going to be a problem for you, we can always look for another inn down the road to accommodate us."

I sure hate to pass up the potential profits such a brisk business would mean. "How many passengers do you have on the bus?"

"There's thirty-five counting myself."

Bill nodded. "Well, if your passengers wouldn't mind having a drink first in our lounge, we could probably begin seating them at," he looked at his watch, "6:45 in about 30 minutes."

John nodded. "You got yourself a deal. I'll have them all unloaded in a couple of minutes." He started to leave, then stopped, looking back at Bill. "Before I take them off the bus, you should throw some rock salt down on the sidewalk outside so no one gets hurt."

Bill nodded and hurried toward the kitchen to hopefully find Ted about clearing the walkway and notifying staff of the impending rush of business.

Chapter 31

Nia leaned back in her chair and glanced up at the clock. *Why am I still here? My shift ended 15 minutes ago. I can't do anything more tonight.* She stood up to leave. The phone rang. Nia looked at it and made a face, debating whether to pick it up. She smiled to herself, shaking her head. *I just can't resist, can I?* She lifted the receiver and sat down on the desk. "Detective D'Amato, Ninth Precinct."

"Hello, detective. Leroy Yazbek. I just received word from dispatch that they heard from the driver of the 676 to Montreal. They've run into a bad northeaster and needed to divert off of Route 89 North to Route 4 West. Because of a downed power line, they are planning to stop at the Vermont Inn in Rutland until it's fixed, and conditions improve."

"That's great!" exclaimed Nia jumping to her feet. She thought for a moment how that must sound. "Well, it's good considering the dangerous driving conditions. Thanks for letting me know, Mr. Yazbek. I'll handle it from here."

"Detective, are you sure the passengers aren't in any danger from this guy?"

"To be honest, we don't even know if our potential suspect is on that bus. But in any event, we'll take every precaution to ensure their safety."

As Nia put down the phone, she tapped on her desk and studied the ceiling, considering a preposterous idea, crazy even by her standards. She recalled that her old partner, a beat cop who had left Boston a dozen years ago and moved his family to the Rutland area, was still stationed there. She called the Rutland police, identified herself, and asked to speak to Jim Walden.

"This is Sergeant Greene. I'm sorry Jim is unavailable. How can I help you, detective?"

Damn. So much for keeping this low-key. Change of plan. "Sergeant, we're investigating a homicide and are looking into the possibility that our suspect may have boarded a Greyhound bus early this afternoon in Boston bound for Montreal. We were just informed that the bus was on Route 4 and learned of down power lines outside of Rutland. They decided to wait for them to be repaired at the Vermont Inn.

"Hmm. What can you tell me about this possible suspect, detective?"

"Not much of a description yet. He's male, probably middle-aged, average build, about six feet, with dark eyes and he may be wearing a baseball hat and winter jacket. If he's on that bus, we have reason to believe that he might be armed, dangerous, and probably nervous about this diversion to the inn."

There was a pause. "That's a lot of 'ifs' detective."

"I wouldn't have called, but this diversion to the inn might complicate apprehending the suspect, if he's on that bus."

"Well detective, I just dispatched Jim to the inn to help locate the wife of the owner who was reported missing about thirty minutes ago."

"Sergeant, I don't think it's such a good idea for Jim to show up at the inn in uniform. If our suspect is there, there's no telling how he might react."

"True. Hold on while I try to raise him."

Lines of concern etched Sergeant Greene's face as he tried to raise Jim on the police radio. "Cruiser one ten, cruiser one ten, this is station one, come in please." A noisy wall of static confirmed that the heavy snow was conspiring to block the repeated hails to the seasoned officer.

"Detective D'Amato. No luck. The storm, along with static from our backup generators, is playing havoc with all of our transmissions outside of a mile or so."

"Damn. Jim could be walking into trouble and never know it. How long will the roads be blocked?"

"I'm guessing at least for another three or four hours or so."

"Is there any other way to keep Jim from walking into a potentially dangerous situation at the inn?

"Well, I could call the inn, but if word gets out, some of the staff might start acting jumpy or looking twice at anyone suspicious." There was a long pause. "I do seem to recall that there was a short-wave radio in the handyman's shop if Ted has it on and he's listening to it. I could try to reach Jim through Ted. But that is a lot of ifs."

"It's worth a try, Sergeant."

"Spencer"

"What?"

"If we're going to be doing some work together, you can call me Spencer."

"Oh. Okay Spencer, and I'm Nia. I'll hang on here while you try the shortwave radio."

Chapter 32

Ted usually left the inn by 6:00 pm unless there was an emergency. Tonight, the heavy snow and blackout would delay his driving the two miles to his 'A' frame cottage until he finished plowing around the cars in the parking lot and they were back up on the power grid. After he parked the snow blower in the shed, he returned to his shop to hang up the keys and turn off a second backup auxiliary generator he'd been testing.

He stopped to look at the picture hanging just above his keys of Megan, Bill, and Ted a few days after they had bought the inn. Ted had planned to retire for good after the inn was sold but then they asked him to stay. He knew the young couple had sold or mortgaged everything to buy the inn and there wasn't much money left over for updates. He reluctantly agreed to stay on and help out until they got their feet under them and things were running smoothly. He'd already been working at the inn for over 10 years and had done more than a lifetime's worth of maintenance and repairs to the place. *That's when they snapped that picture.*

He smiled as he recalled one of his early eye-opening experiences. He was in the middle of a plumbing repair in one of the rooms and needed to work around the times when it was occupied. This led to his first really embarrassing encounter with the amorous occupants of a room who failed to hear his too gentle knockings. He quickly learned the importance of knocking with authority, announcing who he was, waiting, then opening the door partway and shouting, "Maintenance", again before marching into the room.

That reminds me. I'm almost finished with that job in Room 19. He'd already cut and reinforced the opening for a fireplace insert and had a gas line installed with a shutoff valve.

He just needed to finish up installing the insert and connecting the supply and exhaust pipes. He knew that with any luck, the fireplace would be installed within the next couple of days. Then he'd just need to test it, add the tiles, and it would be ready for use by the end of the week.

The short-wave radio in the corner of the shop suddenly crackled with static, startling him out of his reverie.

"Ted, this is Sergeant Greene, over."

He picked up the mic. "Hi, Spencer. What's up?"

"I need you to do me a big favor. Jim Walden is on his way up there, and I need you to intercept him before he gets to the inn. Tell him to contact the station immediately and not go into the inn."

"Why shouldn't he come to the inn?"

"Let's just say we don't want to get one of your guests all riled up."

"Hold on, Spencer. This sounds like something serious, and I think I do need to know about it."

"Ted, we're just trying to be careful. Right now, the fewer people involved, the better. I promise if we need you, you'll be brought up to date on what's going on."

"So, you'd like me to stick around and monitor the short-wave, right?"

"We could really use you on the inside."

"Okay. Then how about telling me what's going on."

Spencer swore under his breath. "Okay. It's *possible* one of the passengers on the bus from Boston is a suspect in a murder investigation." He exaggerated the word 'possible.' "If it's true, and that's a big if, he might be fleeing to Canada and would probably be armed and considered dangerous."

"Don't you think the staff should know about this?"

"Hell no! Not yet. They'll start acting paranoid, then this guy might notice and do something rash. Besides, we don't even know if this guy is on that bus. Let's wait until we know more before making that decision.

"Okay. I guess you're right. I'll head out to intercept Jim and contact you after I talk to him. Do you have a description of this guy"?

"I'm afraid nothing very useful. Male, about six feet, dark eyes, middle-aged and maybe wearing a baseball hat. I'll wait for your call. Good luck. Out."

Ted stood slowly, the microphone still clenched in his hand, feeling the heat from the top of the old ham radio receiver ripple across his face. He walked over to the hook where he hung his fleece-lined coat and muttered *shit* under his breath. He pulled on the coat, pushed open the rear door, and was greeted with a stinging icy blast. He lowered his head and marched out into the storm.

Chapter 33

Benny played with his napkin, using his glass of beer to push it forward and back along the bar. He was unhappy about the delay in getting to Canada. He knew he should have plenty of time to catch a flight out of the country before the police traced the theft of jewels back to him. He looked around at the crowd sitting and standing nearby. He felt out of place in the small bar. The passengers all seemed just a little too loud and animated for his liking. *Fucking money belt is digging into me every time I move. It's driving me crazy. I can't take it off and easily hide it.* He looked down at the Patriot's jacket. *I look like a fucking billboard. I swear people can see the bulge of my gun.* Benny liked to keep his weapon tucked in his waist band where he could pull it out quickly if he needed it. He made a face and gave his head a shake. *Can't do that now wearing this fucking chastity belt. I'll never get to it, zippered up in my pocket.*

Benny unconsciously kept touching the briefcase full of money with his foot. *I need to get up and take a look around this place, just in case.* He looked down. *It might draw unwanted attention if I start carrying this thing around everywhere I go.* He looked up at the bartender. "Hey, bartender, would you watch my briefcase while I go take a leak?"

The bartender looked over from wiping a glass. "Sure. No problem. I'm not going anywhere."

Benny slid off the bar stool and wandered back in the direction of the dining room and stopped. *The dining room has double doors at the back that lead into a kitchen. I bet the kitchen has an entrance out the back.* He turned and walked toward the reception area. *There's two bathrooms and another room down that narrow corridor to the right of the reception*

149

area. He walked past the bathrooms and looked into a spacious game room with a pool table, a number of chairs and small tables, and shelves filled with what looked like puzzles and board games. *No outside exit, but there's a door over there labeled, **Innkeeper Residence**. I suppose if I really needed another way out.* He turned and walked back past the registration counter to two sofas lining the edge of a sitting room area. He stopped and picked up an apple from a fruit bowl on the massive coffee table, appearing to inspect it. He turned his attention to the sitting room. *A fireplace, some chairs, nothing else this way.* He replaced the fruit, then sauntered over to the bay windows that looked out onto the parking area. A tall figure walking briskly along the edge of the driveway and down toward Route 4 caught his attention. He moved closer, squinting. *Now that's odd.* His whispered voice frosted the inside of the window. *Why would anyone be out walking in this weather after dark, heading toward a busy interstate? Huh, maybe I need to check it out and see what's going on.* As he turned to head out the door to the parking lot, Bill's voice echoed from the entrance to the dining room behind him. "Excuse me sir, we have just started to seat folks in the dining room. Would you like to follow me this way?"

Benny turned and hesitated, torn between following the mysterious figure outside, and following Bill into the dining room. He knew it would be hard to explain why he was going outside in a storm. He decided one guy outside on foot couldn't represent that much of a threat. *All this money is making me paranoid.* He replied, "Okay. I'll be right there." He gave a long last look at the disappearing figure out the window.

Chapter 34

Jim Walden loved the outdoors. He moved to Vermont from Boston with his family so that he could take advantage of the excellent winter skiing conditions on some of the nearby peaks. He found most of the police work in the Rutland area pretty routine: traffic accidents, minor vandalism, an occasional runaway, a missing person now and then. His mind started to wander, thinking about the last time he spoke to Megan at the inn. He felt the patrol car begin to slide sideways as it struggled to climb the final hill before the inn. He instinctively wrenched the wheel in the opposite direction, overcorrecting and sending the car skidding across the road, sliding into a drifted wall of white. Jim threw up his arms protectively as the front half of the cruiser plowed into a bank of snow. A soft muffled crunch was followed by an exploding shower of icy crystals raining over the windshield. Jim's head bounced off the steering wheel. He sat stunned for a moment, watching the wipers struggle to push away a new layer of snow. He shook his head, trying to make sense out of what just happened. *Hmm. Not hard enough to deploy the airbags.* He felt a warm trickle leak from a gash in his scalp just above his forehead. He reached up, touching it with the tips of his fingers, grimacing as he inspected the bright red staining the ends of his gloves. *Damn.*

He picked up the mike and called in. He was greeted by a steady hiss of white noise. He sat for a moment considering his options. He tried to open his door and found it unyielding, half buried in snow. The passenger door had buckled and was jammed tight as well. He reflexively turned toward the back seat and smiled as he remembered the protective cage barrier. He tried lowering the power windows on both doors without any luck. Jim muttered one of his favorite phrases. *Well here's another fine mess you've gotten me into Ollie.*

He briefly debated whether to stay in the car and try to raise headquarters or break a window and walk the rest of the way to the inn. He fought his first impulse to break a window and instead picked up the mike again to contact the station. "Rutland HQ this is cruiser one ten, come in." There was a faint reply overlaid with heavy static. He repeated the call again. There was another wall of static with something not quite understandable in the background. He took a deep breath and sat for a moment considering how long he should wait imprisoned in his cruiser. He knew he was never very patient when he had to wait. *The longer I sit here, the less chance we'll have of finding Megan alive. I guess it's time to go with plan B.*

He carefully removed his gun from the holster. He shifted over toward the window on the passenger's side and swung hard toward the center of the glass. To his surprise, the gun butt bounced off the glass, leaving only a scratch in the center. He tried again with the same result. He wondered aloud if he was doomed to be a prisoner in his own cruiser until help came along. He briefly flirted with the thought of trying to fix the power windows. *I can't be found sitting here unable to get out of my cruiser. I'll never hear the end of it. Screw this!* He swung his feet up into the air, tucking his body into a fetal position and drove both feet into the side window. The glass exploded out into thousands of small fragments. *I'm going to catch hell for this back at the station.*

Jim grabbed his oak nightstick, poked out the remaining pieces of glass. He crawled out of the window, tumbling head first into the knee-high snow. He stood up, wiped the snow off his face, hair, and uniform and then surveyed the damage to the cruiser. The front end had undoubtedly sustained some body damage though it was difficult to tell from looking at it half buried in the snow. The side window was history, and the inside of the cruiser was fast filling with snow. He turned and started walking the remaining half-mile to the inn.

Jim pulled his collar up to protect his neck from the blasts of cold and snow that seemed determined to push their way inside his jacket. As he started to turn onto Cream Hill Road, which ran along the side of the inn property, he spotted a tall figure walking quickly towards him waving. Jim stopped, surprised to see anyone out in this weather. He recognized Ted, from his powerful frame and crop of sandy hair that stuck out from the top of his parka. Jim shouted above the howling wind, "Ted, you shouldn't be out searching on a nasty night like this."

Ted looked at him confused. "What? Searching? No. I'm here to stop you from going to the inn. Where's your cruiser?"

Jim shook his head. "The short version is I plowed it into a snow bank."

"Are you okay?" Ted squinted, looking at Jim more closely. "Hey, you're bleeding," he pointed, "there on your forehead."

"Yeah. I did that when I crashed into a snowbank. It's nothing too serious. What else is going on that has you coming out here to meet me?"

"Not here. It's a long story. I'll bring you around the back way and fill you in. We need to keep a low profile."

Jim started to ask about Megan, thought better of it, and fell in behind Ted. He watched him walk around the side of the inn, wading through a drift-covered path of snow, then disappear into the darkness. He followed pushing through the drift and around the back to Ted's workshop directly behind the inn. They were both out of breath as they stood just inside the door, pounding their feet to shake off the caked snow. Ted threw his jacket onto the broken wicker chair in the corner and turned to face Jim. "Spencer called me on the ham radio. He's been trying to reach you in the cruiser about a possible situation here at the inn.

Jim cocked his head, speaking slowly. "What kind of situation?" he asked with a growing look of concern.

"I think I'll let your boss fill you in," Jim replied picking up the microphone. "VI to Rutland police."

There was a brief blast of static followed by, "Hi Ted, this is Spencer. Is Jim there?"

Ted handed Jim the microphone. "Spencer, this is Jim. What's going on?"

Ted watched Jim's face darken, nodding in agreement as Sergeant Spencer quickly filled him in on the details. "Yes, sir. I understand."

Ted cocked his head puzzled as Spencer asked Jim if there was any word about Megan. "No sir. I haven't had a chance to ask. But it doesn't look like Bill informed the staff yet."

Ted reached out and held Jim's arm. "Wait a minute! What the hell's going on with Megan?

Spencer answered. "Ted, Bill called to say his wife was missing in the woods. That was a couple of hours ago before this business about a possible suspect on the bus came up. So I don't believe they're related. That was the original reason why Jim was dispatched to the inn. It appears Bill decided not to tell any of the staff about this and I think we should keep it that way. We'll have to wait for the storm to subside before we can start any search for her. Let's just focus on this possible suspect for now."

After talking it over, Spencer decided as a precaution, that Jim should pose as one of the wait staff and Ted would stay close by the dining room, bringing in wood and tending the fireplace. They agreed Bill and the staff would need to be told of the situation to avoid a potentially disastrous greeting. Before signing off, Spencer promised to keep them informed of any new developments regarding getting additional help to the inn.

Ted helped him clean up the gash on his head in a bathroom off the kitchen. Luckily it had stopped bleeding. Jim found it could easily be hidden by combing down some of his hair. Ted found extra pants, shirt and jacket in the kitchen for Jim to wear that were made for someone about the same build, but shorter. Jim struggled to push the pants low enough on his hips to cover his ankles. He gave Ted a frustrated look. "I look more like a refugee from a Salvation Army store than a waiter at a country inn.

Ted suppressed a smile. "I'll go find Bill and give him the news."

Chapter 35

Nia, now officially off duty, propped her feet up on the desk and drifted into an uneasy sleep. A hulking, menacing figure with two hairy arms was holding her down, her arms pinned tightly. She squirmed, frantically trying to reach her weapon. From out of sight came two more arms, like cold venomous snakes. They began to inch their way, one sliding between the buttons on her shirt, a second one thrusting smoothly down the front of her pants. A harsh buzzing sound startled her awake instantly. She gasped for air, momentarily disorientated by a reoccurring nightmare from when her mother was attacked. She launched her hand toward the desk and fumbled with the receiver, picking it up on the third ring. "Detective D'Amato."

"Nia, Spencer. I have Jim working undercover at the inn. But we are still flying blind here. We don't know much about who we are looking for or even if the suspect is on that bus. Also, it looks like it'll be at least another four hours before the roads are clear enough for that bus to leave."

"Sergeant, I mean Spencer, I finished work half an hour ago and I got the next couple of days off and would like to visit Rutland. I might be able to lend a hand identifying"

Spencer cut her off in mid-sentence. "Hold on. While we can always use an extra pair of hands on a case like this, I don't think with this snow storm..." Static filled the line while Nia heard the sergeant swearing into the phone. The receiver on the other end went dead.

Nia sat for a moment, one hand still resting on the phone. Her lips were drawn into a reflective crease. *Am I really considering this? I have the weekend off, but I probably wouldn't get there in time to be of any help. And my Toyota Camry is no match for these wintery conditions.* She stood up, biting the inside of her cheek. She started to walk slowly out of the assignment room, oblivious to the bustle of activity happening around her, lost in a series of calculations.

Most of the day shift had left for the evening, and a new, smaller crop of detectives was sorting through their assignments. Near a bank of windows toward the front of the room, Joe Donovan, a recent retiree, had just finished cleaning out his file cabinet and was putting some final items into a cardboard box.

Making up her mind, Nia approached the gray-haired man taking a picture down from the wall. "Donovan. I have a favor to ask."

He turned; his steel blue eyes were full of surprise. "D'Amato. I thought you were day shift?" He glanced up at the clock noting it was after 6:00 p.m. "Did you get demoted?" His weathered face broke into a broad grin.

"Oh, you know me. I'm just a demotion waiting to happen. And why are *you* still here? You should be on a beach somewhere warm and sunny."

He shook his head. "My timing has always been lousy. That's why I'm in no hurry to go home. I'm getting too familiar with frozen dinners and cable TV with nothing to watch. What kind of favor?"

"You still own that four-wheel drive jeep?"

"Yup. Something wrong with your car? Do you need a lift?"

"No. I'd like to swap cars with you. I need to chase down a lead I've been working on and in this weather, I can't afford to get stuck."

"What case are we talking about?"

"That jewelry heist and shooting earlier today off of Washington Street."

"So, where do you need to go in the city?"

"Ah. It's a little outside of the city."

"Okay. Do you want to tell me where?"

Nia hesitated, knowing that Donovan might balk at her taking his car to Vermont. "Rutland."

He looked incredulous. "As in Rutland, Vermont?"

"Yeah." She rushed to fill in more details. "Listen. Jim Walden might be in danger. You remember me talking about Jim. He was my partner back when we shared a squad car in Hyde Park a dozen years back."

"Yes. I do seem to remember you telling me Jim saved your bacon during a domestic violence incident."

Nia nodded in agreement adding, "So that's why I feel I…"

Donovan interrupted, holding up one hand. "Why you feel you need to go rushing up there alone, driving into a snowstorm to help him. D'Amato, have you *really* thought this out?"

"Okay. I know it sounds a little rash. But Jim may be walking into a real mess. We don't know for sure who the murderer is. And I have the weekend off. So, I figured since I know some of the suspects, if I can get up there in time, I could make a positive ID."

"I'd say more than a little rash and who else besides me knows you are planning to go and help?"

"Well."

"I thought so." He shook his head, looking down, and then up at Nia. "I'll probably regret this, but I'll let you take my car on one condition." He paused. "I come with it."

"Look, Donovan. I appreciate the offer to help, but I can't get you involved in this case."

Donovan put his hands on the desk and looked hard at Nia. "That's the offer, detective. Take it or leave it."

Nia drew a deep breath and knew she had no other choice. "Okay. But I'm planning on leaving from here."

Donovan smiled. "Sounds fine to me. My car's in the lot in back. And it just so happens it's full of gas and ready to go."

Chapter 36

Nia grabbed her coat, checked the piece in her shoulder holster, and followed Donovan out of the squad room. As they approached his jeep, Donovan offered, "I'll take the first shift driving. Okay?"

The driving's going to get a lot rougher as we get further north and west. "Sure. When the going gets tough, I'll take over." She looked over the hood at Donovan and grinned before sliding into the passenger side. As the jeep negotiated around stalled cars littering the side streets leading to Boston's newly depressed central artery, Nia stared at the steady drum of wind-driven snow on the windshield. She was sure the suspect was one of the names on her list. If she could see the passengers on that bus, she'd know immediately if one of them was responsible for the robbery and murder.

Using care and skill honed from years of driving a 4-wheel drive car through difficult conditions, Donovan made his way to one of the many entrances to Boston's underground mile-long artery. After a brief reprieve from the relentless snow, they emerged out of the tunnel and were immediately buffeted by fierce cross-winds and heavy sheets of snow.

"I think Bette is going to get a real workout tonight."

"Bette?"

"I always give my cars a name. That's what I call this beauty." He slapped the dashboard above the radio. "She's never let me down yet. Of course, it's been a while since we've been through nasty weather."

"That's very reassuring. I think", replied Nia skeptically.

Donovan looked over at Nia. "This might be a good time to catch a little shut-eye before it's your turn to drive."

Nia nodded. "Sounds like a plan." She sunk lower in her seat and closed her eyes. Her stomach growled. It reminded her the last time she ate a really fine meal. She was with her boyfriend Chris, last spring. *Had it really been last May, seven months since he broke up with me? I was clueless of how tired he was having to always wait for me.* Nia made a disgruntled face, hoping Donovan wouldn't notice. *Some detective. I wouldn't show up for a date and then I'd eventually call, always with the same lame excuse. On those occasions that I did show up, I was really late. I guess at some point, he just had enough. What I found frustrating was he didn't even want to talk about it. I guess he knew he would always come second to my police work.*

And then there was our last evening. I thought he would understand, like all the other times. That's what I liked about Chris. He didn't complain, seemed willing to wait, and then he'd forgive me. That last night he had let himself into my apartment and was waiting for me. I entered, apologizing, not looking at him as I tossed my hat and jacket on a nearby chair. Then I turned and looked up into his angry face and froze. I didn't immediately understand what was wrong. I started to speak, but he held up his hand as he walked across the tiny living room; his words hit me like ice water.

"I can't go on like this. I know you love your police work more than anything and I respect that. But I want more than you'll ever be able to give me. I know I'm being selfish, and I *am* sorry. But I need to end this for my own sanity. Goodbye Nia."

I couldn't believe what I was hearing and tried to stop him. "Wait. You can't just leave like this. Can't we talk about this, Chris? Please?"

He shook his head. "I know. I'm not being fair to you. And I'm sorry." *He threw my key down on the coffee table. His face was deeply sad, his angry eyes rimmed with tears. He turned and slammed the door to the apartment. I dropped to my knees feeling flushed, doubled over by a wave of nausea. I couldn't understand how I missed or ignored Chris's building frustration and anger. I slumped down on the sofa, hugging my knees. I kept replaying scenes from our two-year relationship, seeing too late all those little warning signs.*

I tried to reconnect with Chris once or twice without success but wasn't sure if that was what I really wanted. I knew he had a hard time expressing how he was feeling but didn't understand why all of a sudden he had enough and didn't want to talk about it. I spent a lot of time feeling guilty, knowing that I missed lots of clues, being too wrapped up in my own work to notice.

*That all stopped on the day I went to a Red Sox game in September with a group of cops from my precinct. During the seventh inning stretch, the jumbotron showed a happy couple that had just got engaged. My jaw dropped. It was Chris and a smiling blonde, excitedly waving her ring finger and waving to the cheering crowd. Guess **he** didn't waste any time moving on.* She turned toward the snow coated window. *I wonder if maybe Chris had already met his future fiancé while we were still together. I know I'm not getting much shut-eye replaying this disaster movie.*

Nia had recently turned 37 and knew it was increasingly hard to meet someone new through the usual dating venues like clubs and bars and singles parties. She was increasingly conscious of her age around all the early twenty somethings and found herself uncomfortable with the nervous laughter, phony pickup lines, and unfamiliar music. The excitement of that life had evaporated while she was busy pursuing her detective's badge. *I suppose, I have my work to keep me busy. But I feel really lonely sometimes.*

***

Most people had left the city early trying to beat the storm, so by 6:45 pm, traffic was light, moving steadily at reduced speeds. They managed to stay in a recently cleared travel lane through northeastern Massachusetts and into southern New Hampshire as far as Manchester. As they approached the exit for Route 89 North, Nia looked at her watch. "It's 8:15 and it looks like they've cleared the accident from the off-ramp ahead." A heavy layer of salt and sand was fast disappearing under an onslaught of snow. "I'm done napping. How about I take a turn at the wheel?"

"The next place I can turn off and get an oversized cup of coffee, it's all yours."

"Add a couple of donuts to that order and you can name your price."

He laughed. "Better be careful what you wish for detective." Donovan found a Dunkin' Donuts coffee shop open in a strip mall just off the interstate outside of Hanover, New Hampshire. A teenage girl with pink hair and a half-shaven head was refilling a coffee mug for a trucker. He had a handlebar mustache and a mane of snow-flecked graying hair hanging over his denim collared jacket. Spying Donovan waiting at the counter, he turned and said, "Where you headed?"

Donovan replied, "Over to Rutland on Route 4."

"The road up that way is still in tough shape. I hear the plows are having a hard time clearing some of the sections west of Killington. It may not be passable till midnight or later", the man replied.

"It's pretty important we get there in the next few hours. I guess I'll just have to take my chances."

The trucker nodded adding, "I hear you. Well, take it slow, buddy."

Donovan returned to the jeep with donuts and two large coffees. He found Nia already sitting in the driver's seat. "I think we'll need these for the next part of the trip if that trucker's info is right." Joe related the coffee shop conversation to a worried Nia. Seeing the look on her face, Joe added, "Of course if you'd like me to drive."

Nia's face broke into a broad smile, "Not on your life. I've had my two-hour nap, I've got coffee and donuts, and I'm good to go for the rest of the trip. How long do you think it'll take to reach the inn?"

"Given the distance and the mountains ahead, I'd say it usually takes about an hour and a half to two hours. Tonight, it could easily be three or more. So, it's 8:40 pm. With a little luck, we might make it by eleven-thirty."

Nia made a face. "That late huh? Let's get going." She backed out of the space and carefully made her way to the on-ramp for Route 89 North. Donovan looked behind them. They were the only car visible on the two-lane highway. Nia followed a deeply rutted set of tracks in the right lane and was able to keep the jeep moving as fast as she dared until she approached a set of dim red tail lights moving very slowly through the snow just ahead. Nia grimaced commenting, "If they're going to be on this road for long, we won't get there till morning."

"The left lane looks totally unusable." remarked Donovan leaning over to take a look. "Wait a minute. Got an idea." He opened the glove compartment and rummaged through a pile of papers. "Here we are." He pulled out a red plastic light with a suction cup on the bottom and switched it on. He placed it on the dashboard as the red rotating light jumped to life and filled the interior of the car with a pulsing red glow.

Almost immediately, the snow-shrouded car in front rolled to a stop. The jeep carefully crept around it, fish-tailing slightly. They bounced back into the right lane and slowly built up speed.

"Thank God for your toys.", quipped Nia. "Let's hope we don't encounter too many more cars like that."

They spent the next hour riding in silence as Nia's thoughts drifted to her former partner, Jim Walden. They both worked together in Boston a dozen years ago. In those days, Nia had been a bit rash, ready to charge into any situation. However, under Jim's steadying influence, she matured from an impulsive rookie into an experienced, seasoned veteran. *Yeah. A seasoned veteran who still makes rash decisions.* A bump roused Nia from her thoughts as they crossed the Vermont border. She slowed the car to a crawl as they inched along the off-ramp onto Route 4 just outside Quechee Gorge.

Part 4: Deadly Guest

Chapter 37

Bill repeatedly glanced at the clock as he passed through the kitchen and by the long food preparation counter opposite the two massive ovens. It had been over a half hour since he phoned Spencer at the station. He wondered aloud what was keeping the patrol car. Steven looked up in the middle of preparing his boneless breast of chicken stuffed with Macintosh apples and raisins. "What's that, Bill? Are you expecting the police?"

Startled, Bill stammered, "Ah, no I was just thinking out loud."

Steven continued to stare at Bill, looking momentarily confused, before shrugging and turning back to pound the chicken. Bill turned and quickly fled the kitchen in embarrassment. *Damn! I'm making my thoughts public. I have to be more careful. Guests will start to notice.* He bumped into Cindy as he entered the dining room.

She saw the concerned look on his face and touched his arm. "You okay?"

His first impulse was to shout, "No!", but checked himself and instead replied, "Been better."

Cindy started to reply, decided against it, and continued into the kitchen.

Benny picked at his salad as he shifted uncomfortably in his chair, looking around the crowded dining room at the mix of skiers and bus passengers. He noticed that at one table a young couple talked quietly over a bottle of red wine silhouetted by the flames from a massive stone fireplace that occupied half of one wall in the dining room. He had the odd feeling that the man had been looking at him, but every time he looked up, the couple seemed completely enthralled with each other.

Dave first noticed the movements of the sharp-featured man from the bus as the couple was being led into the dining room. He was sitting alone at a table for one in a candle-lit corner. He seemed to be scanning the room, glancing from side to side, tense, ready for what? He only half listened to Heidi as he played with his pork medallions. As she chatted about their misadventures and numerous spills on the slopes of Killington, he wondered what events would drive a man such as this, out of his element. It was apparent he was uneasy in these north country surroundings and was not dressed for any outdoor activities, Once or twice the man looked up quickly and almost caught Dave staring in his direction.

Heidi and Dave finished their dinner and slipped quietly from their table walking toward the lounge. Dave casually glanced at Benny and their eyes locked for one brief moment. In Benny's mind, this was no chance encounter. The man knew, somehow, something about him. Up till now, he felt frustrated, unable to take control of the situation like he had done back in the alley. He trusted those instincts that had got him safely out of the city. Now he knew what he needed to do next.

He slowly stood, preparing to leave his half-finished meal. He glanced down at his briefcase, hesitated, and then followed Heidi and Dave out of the restaurant. He paused in the lounge, feigning interest in an old photo of the inn on the wall. He watched Dave walk up to the coffee table grabbing a Macintosh apple from the brightly colored ceramic bowl. Heidi stood by the parson's table near the door to the rooms playing with a pile of sample dinner menus. Benny waited for the right moment.

"Dave, I feel like going up to the room."

Dave felt a surge of blood quicken his pulse and an unmistakable pressure in his groin. He looked up and tried to act casual as he replied bowing, "Your wish."

Heidi gave a laughing reply. "Is my command." She led the way up the stairs toward their room.

As soon as the couple left the sitting room, Benny walked briskly to the stairs leading up to the rooms. Heidi and Dave were oblivious to the man a half dozen steps behind them as Bill unlocked the door. Benny ran the last few steps and caught the door with his foot, forcing it back open. Dave whirled, startled at the intrusion behind him. He started to say, "What the hell!" He froze when he saw the gun pointed at his chest.

"Don't try to be a hero and you and your friend won't get hurt, Buddy."

"It's Dave. What do you want, money?"

"Money is one thing I don't want." He kicked the door closed. "Both of you sit down over there." He motioned toward the bed with the gun. "We are going to have a little chat."

Heidi tightly clutched Dave's hand, watching the menacing man with the large gun. Benny quickly surveyed the room. He walked over to the hook on the bathroom door and took the tie from the terry cloth bathrobe.

"You honey. Hand me the room key, then take this and tie lover boy's hands behind his back nice and tight. Heidi hesitated, looking at Dave. Dave whispered, "It's okay." He nodded. "Go ahead, Heidi."

"Heidi, nice name. Wrap it around a couple of times. Now pull it tight and make a knot. One more. Good. Now, Dave, sit on the floor against the bedpost." Dave edged off the bed glaring at Benny, then awkwardly knelt, rolling on his side, finally sitting against the bedpost. "Okay Heidi, take off his belt and tie his hands to the bottom." She hesitated, knowing that with each step she was making it harder for them to escape. He cocked the gun. "Let's go, let's go. You wouldn't want your friend's brains all over the bed sheets? I've already done one fool today, two won't make any difference."

Heidi knelt down and took off Dave's belt. He whispered, "It's okay. I love you." Tears began to spill down her face. She pulled the leather tight and set the catch to lock it into place.

Benny waved the gun at her, gesturing toward the overstuffed chair next to the window. "Go sit over there in the corner and don't move." He inspected Heidi's work. "Nice, very nice." He stood then sat down near Dave on the bed. "So, Dave, how did you know about me? You some kind of cop?"

"What? A cop. You must be crazy."

"Maybe I am crazy. Crazy enough to make you watch me having wild sex with your hot girlfriend over there. Dave's face turned red as he strained against the tie and belt holding him firmly against the bed.

"If you touch her I'll"

"You'll what? Kill me. Hmmm. Well, I can see you're pretty dumb. Maybe even more dumb than a cop."

Dave mumbled, "I'm a shrink."

Benny let out a small shriek that startled both Dave and Heidi. "A shrink. Oh, that's good. Really? A shrink. So, tell me, Dave, the shrink, how come you were so interested in watching me downstairs?"

Dave pursed his lips and shook his head. Benny jumped off the bed, ran behind Dave grabbing his hair and put the cold metal barrel against his temple. "No, well okay. Say goodbye to Heidi."

As he cocked the hammer, Heidi screamed, "No, please! Tell him Dave or I will."

"Ah. The young lady knows as well. Maybe she'll be more inclined to talk to me." Benny let go of Dave's hair giving his head a shove against the bedpost. A small trickle of blood oozed from a cut above his temple and ran down the side of his face. He started to walk toward the chair and heard Dave exclaim, "Okay, okay."

Benny whirled around. "A change of heart. I'm all ears."

Dave begrudgingly began to tell of their dinner conversation. "I make it a habit of noticing people and how they behave. I was curious how someone, dressed the way you do, would choose to head up North. It just seemed out of character. I tried to be unobtrusive in my observations. I guess I failed."

"Yeah. I guess you did. Well, I can't just saunter out of here and leave you two lovebirds alone can I?"

Dave turned and tried to exchange a worried glance with Heidi. Benny walked over to the closet rifling through the hanging clothes. "Let's see. You brought your own bathrobes. How sweet. He took two more ties. These should do it." He walked over to the bed and patted the mattress. "Come over and make yourself comfortable, Heidi." Heidi stood, closed her eyes and shuddered, then walked to the side of the bed. "Okay. Now lie down with your feet spread and your hands over your head." Heidi obediently complied. "This is just to make sure you don't go doing anything foolish." Dave struggled against the belt holding him to the bedpost as Benny tied the bathrobe cord around her wrists, knotted it twice and then fastened it to the back of the bed. He slipped a Swiss Army knife from his pocket and cut the other cord in two, then did the same with each leg.

"Oh, I almost forgot." Benny walked into the bathroom and selected one of the long terry bath towels. and cut the towel into three, long, four-inch wide strips. He carried the strips out into the room over his arm, swung one of the strips over Heidi's head and across her lips forcing it into her mouth and tying it. "That's just so we don't get any ideas about hollering for help." He then walked over to Dave and repeated the procedure gagging him as well, giving the knot an extra tug. He then started to use the last strip to tie Dave's feet together. As Benny crouched over, Dave kicked him full in the face sending him sprawling across the room. A trickle of blood oozed from one of his nostrils. He sat stunned for a moment and shook his head, wiping a finger across his nose and inspecting the bloody streak. His face twisted into a scowl. "Bad move, asshole."

He walked to the side of the bed grabbing the gun by the barrel and swung it down across Dave's head. Heidi gave a muffled scream as Dave's body twisted violently sideways as he slumped forward, unconscious against his restraints. Benny reached over and grabbed a pillow, smearing the blood trickling from his nose across the white linen. He tied Dave's legs together, pulling the knots extra tight. "And if they don't find you soon dickhead, you'll be dragging your ass around in a wheelchair, cause your feet won't be working anymore."

He walked over to Heidi. "*You* aren't going to get any bright ideas, are you?" Heidi looked with a tear-stained face and slowly shook her head. "Maybe while your boyfriend is taking a nap, you and I can get to know each other a little better." Heidi closed her eyes praying the nightmare would end.

Sounds floated into the room from the corridor. Benny and Heidi both looked at the door and then at each other. "Don't even think about it," he hissed. From outside the door, a couple was discussing their delicious desert punctuated by the sound of a room key repeatedly missing the door lock. Benny realized with a start that he left a half-eaten meal in the dining room and knew he needed to return to the dining room, or the staff might begin to wonder what happened to him.

He checked the knots on Heidi's ankles and hands and then moved down to check Dave's who was still leaning forward, unconscious. He stood up and looked at Heidi's tear-stained, wide-eyed face. He pointed at her. "Do not make a sound…or you'll never see your boyfriend alive again. Heidi's head slumped to her chest. Benny turned and walked to the door. He stopped and surveyed the room before he opened it. He quietly slipped out and closed the door. He noted with satisfaction that the hallway was deserted.

He stopped outside the empty room next to Heidi and Dave's. A small sign hung on the door: ***Under Construction— Do Not Enter***. *What have we here?* He slipped into the room and fumbled for the light switch. Immediately to his left was a large hole in the wall. *Waiting for the installation of what?* He walked over and stuck his head in the unfinished gas fireplace. *Already has a gas shutoff valve with a plastic nipple at the end and exhaust pipes. Only needs the insert to be installed.* He looked around the room and smiled. *I shouldn't need to use it, but who knows?*

He left the room and descended the steep stairs to the sitting room where two couples were deep in conversation about their delay. He passed up the opportunity to eavesdrop and continued through the lounge to his table in the dining room.

He breathed a sigh of relief as he slipped into his seat, his foot nudging the briefcase leaning against the table leg. He looked up and noticed Ted carefully placing three-foot lengths of split oak down onto a pile of hot glowing embers. When he was finished, Ted continued to stare down at the fire for a moment. *I wonder if he is just preoccupied with the storm or worried about something else. I know he hasn't once glanced over in my direction.* He looked around the dining room. *No one else seems to have noticed or cared that I've been gone.* He smiled. He was feeling very good about his apparent invisibility.

Chapter 38

Leroy Yazbek sat lost in thought, slowly drawing on his cigarette He spoke to the lazy expanding cloud of smoke billowing out, and away, dissolving into nothingness. *So this detective is searching for a killer who just might,* he raised a hand, *be on one of our Greyhound buses. I can still see her fine figure leaving my office, disappearing in that never-ending tide of people that's always rushing by just outside the door. I did want to contact the driver and let him know. But she warned me not to do that. And the detective may be right. I might do more harm than good.*

Leroy liked to unwind at the end of his shift on most days by sitting quietly in the back of his office. He'd hang an OFFICE CLOSED sign outside the door, close his eyes, and lose himself in the throaty saxophone of Lester Young playing in the background. *Yes sir. Today has been a most unusual day. First, that detective comes in and tells me there might be a murder suspect on the bus. Nosey Marge made sure our small staff all knew about it. So first I had to calm that uproar. And then there was that flurry of police activity just outside the terminal because of a stabbing. Despite their good intentions not to interfere with any of the regular bus business, the police still cordoned off a large area with yellow tape, disrupting all the foot traffic around the terminal. Yes sir. Today was one of those days.*

Yazbek kept mulling over the words of the detective. *The passengers will be fine, and the police will take every precaution to ensure their safety. Can I believe her? And what about the driver? I keep thinking about what she said before she left. We request that you do not try to contact the driver with any additional information. It may just make matters worse. But I feel personally responsible for that driver's safety as well as those of his passengers.* He couldn't decide whether to contact the driver or follow her directive. *If John knows he might have a passenger who's a murder suspect, he could start acting differently, tipping off the suspect and endangering everyone at the inn. If I remember correctly, John is quick to laugh but also can be provoked to anger. There's no telling how he will react to this new information. On the other hand, if he is caught unaware and the suspect acts irrationally, a lot of innocent people might get hurt.* He looked up at the ceiling, weighing what he should or should not do, while the dying notes of "Almost Like Being in Love" echoed into silence.

***

The phone at the receptionist's desk at the inn rang with irritating urgency. On the fourth ring, Cindy reached over the counter and snatched it up. "Good evening, Vermont Inn may I help you?"

"Hi, I'm trying to reach John Doherty, the driver of the Greyhound bus. It's important that I speak with him. This is his supervisor, Leroy Yazbek."

Hold on Mr. Yazbek, I'll get him for you. Cindy briskly walked into the bar and announced in a booming voice, "John Doherty. John Doherty, you have a phone call".

Ted had brought in extra wood from outside and was walking through the rear door into the kitchen. He froze when he heard Cindy's announcement, worried about who might be contacting the bus driver and for what reason. But he was more concerned about how a possible murder suspect might react to the announcement.

Benny had just raised a forkful of salad to his mouth when he heard the receptionist make an announcement that the driver had a phone call. Could it be from the police inquiring about his passengers? Would it look too suspicious if he made his way to the bathroom at the same time the driver was going to pick up the phone call? He decided he needed to take that chance as he slipped out of his seat and made his way to the bathroom adjacent to the reception area.

John heard his name as he sat at the end of the polished bar, clearly audible over the excited buzz in the lounge. As he pushed his way through the milling passengers to the reception window, he wondered who would be trying to reach him at this late hour. Cindy pointed to the receiver lying on its side next to the silver push bell. He picked up the phone. "John Doherty."

"John, I'm glad I caught you. Leroy Yazbek. "

"Leroy, what are you ..."

"Just listen. I tried to reach you on your cell, but the service must be screwed up in this weather. There may be a guy on the bus that is a suspect in a robbery and murder here in Boston. He's armed and probably wouldn't hesitate to plug whoever gets in his way."

"How do you know all this?"

"The police have been all over this place. They aren't even sure the guy is on your bus. And I wasn't supposed to call you, but I figured you ought to know. You should steer clear of anybody suspicious, but you should know what you might be dealing with. I'm sure the police will be in touch, but who knows how long that will be with these weather conditions."

"Jesus, I think I might have tangled with the guy earlier."

"You were lucky he didn't blow your head off."

"Leroy, I guess I owe you one."

"Just make sure you stick around long enough for me to collect it."

"I'll plan to do that, Thanks."

"Watch your back and try to keep cool."

"Shouldn't be too hard in this blizzard. Thanks."

There was a click and the line returned to a dial tone as John stood motionless, his face a mask of concern. He slowly reached over to replace the phone and missed the cradle, his mind racing, a million miles away. He turned back to the lounge preoccupied with the terrible weight of this new knowledge, oblivious to the noise and commotion swirling around him.

Benny listened through a partially open bathroom door. He gathered that the driver was being warned by someone from the company and grinned at the thought that the driver suspected Finch was their suspect. Benny figured it wouldn't be hard to keep Finch agitated, and in the spotlight, as a thin smile played on his lips. He waited for the driver to return to the lounge, killing time washing his hands with foamy soap and hot water before making his way back to the dining room.

Chapter 39

Ted could feel the beads of sweat on his forehead as stopped to hear the announcement, before entering the dining room with another armload of wood. *First, I need to tell Bill about the murder suspect and all that had happened. Jim is still waiting for his signal to appear as one of the wait staff. And now, the bus driver is probably being filled in on a possible murder suspect on his bus.* Ted piled the wood in the iron hoop next to the fireplace. He then returned to the kitchen and found Bill talking to the head chef over by the two massive ovens.

The white hat bobbed as the chef explained with animated gestures about what entrees were no longer available. "So that means we've run out of two of our ten entrees and three others are running low. I never anticipated this kind of…"

Ted broke in, "Excuse me, we have an emergency, and I need to talk to Bill."

Bill swung around, a look of horror etched on his face. "My God, it's Megan, isn't it? She was missing outside in the storm. I called the sheriff hours ago, but they can't get through, and it's too dark to go searching now."

Ted shook his head, "I'm really sorry Bill, but it's not about Megan. We need to talk in private."

Steven watched them walk into a small office at the back of the kitchen exclaiming, "And I thought I had problems with the menu."

Ted closed the office door and filled Bill in on the murder suspect who might be on the bus and Jim posing as one of the waiters.

A look of disbelief crossed Bill's face as he shook his head. "My God, what else can go wrong today." He turned and promptly left the office to tell his staff to ignore the 'new' waiter. Ted went to get Jim so that he could float among the patrons at the bar.

He found Jim pacing nervously back and forth in the cluttered workshop. "Are we all set, Ted?"

Ted nodded. "Well, I told him. It should be okay to bring you up to the entrance to the dining room. Oh, and the bus driver just got a phone call, probably from the office in Boston. I'm guessing he's been told about the possible murder suspect on his bus."

"I think we'll need to talk to him to make sure he doesn't decide to act on his own."

They left the workshop and walked to the rear entrance of the kitchen. Jim shook off a light coating of snow and checked the piece hidden inside his jacket. Jim turned to Ted. "Watch for anything that doesn't look right, or anyone who looks nervous. I'll go hang out in the lounge and help with clearing tables and carrying trays of dirty dishes to the kitchen. You should keep working around the dining room, bringing in firewood, tending the fire, and listening for any ham radio messages from Spencer."

"Bussing, Jim. It's called bussing trays."

Jim smirked and shook his head, leaving the kitchen and heading into the lounge. A large blonde woman in a faux fur coat that had a slightly damp gamey smell came up to Jim and said in a slurred voice, "I'll have another one of these."

Jim, forgetting his role replied, "What?"

The woman continued to push her glass at him repeating, "Are you deaf? Fill it up. Fill it up again, Jose."

Jim recovered in time to take the glass, walk over to the bar, and ask for another one of 'these.' The bartender, having witnessed the encounter, gave Jim an amused look saying, "No problemo, Jose."

John fidgeted with his drink, uncomfortable with his new information. He spied Bill walking through the lounge and came to a hasty decision. He slid off the stool, catching Bill by the arm. "I need to talk to you."

Bill, not looking at him, replied, "I'm really quite busy."

John tersely responded, "It's *critical*."

Bill stopped and looked at the anxious face of the driver. He nodded. "Okay. Follow me."

Bill walked into the small office behind the reception window and turned to face the driver. "What's this all about?"

John looked around to make sure no one was within earshot and loudly whispered, "I've been told I may have a murder suspect on the bus. And he may be armed and dangerous." To his surprise, Bill nodded.

"I just found out. Stay here. There are a couple of men you need to meet."

Ted had returned to the lounge to confer with Jim. Bill left the bus driver standing in the office and motioned with his head for the two men to join him. As they entered the office, Bill introduced the bus driver. "Ted and Jim, I'd like you to meet John Doherty, the driver of the Greyhound bus."

Jim stepped forward and shook his hand. "I'm Officer Jim Walden. I'm here to keep an eye on things in case the suspect *was* on your bus." He turned to Ted. "Ted is assisting me in that effort, Mr. Doherty."

Ted nodded. "And I understand you received a phone call?"

"Yes, it was from my supervisor." He looked around lowering his voice. "He warned me about a passenger that might be on my bus. I guess he's a suspect in a robbery and murder investigation in Boston."

Jim turned to Ted. "I wonder how many other people know about this secret?"

John continued in a rush. "You know, I have a passenger on the bus who went ballistic when he heard about the delay. I've been watching him. His name is Norman Finch. You'll find him sitting alone in the dining room stabbing a piece of meat."

Jim had been listening intently to the driver. His description matched what little they knew about the suspect. His mind raced with possibilities none of which made the job of capturing the suspect any easier. "Thank you, John. You have been a great help. It's important to try not to agitate him in any way."

"I seem to do that without even trying."

As Ted watched the bus driver walk away, he turned and asked Jim in a subdued voice. "Okay, so what do we know?"

Jim ticked off on his fingers what they had learned. "Well, we know that there may be a murder suspect that boarded this bus in Boston and that the murder is believed to be related to a jewelry robbery. The bus driver thinks that the guy at the table nearest the fireplace is our suspect, because he got bent out of shape when he found out that the bus was being diverted from Montreal to the inn."

Ted suddenly stood up. "I think we should go and quietly persuade Mr."

"Finch," Jim offered.

"Mr. Finch to come with us and discuss this *unavoidable* delay."

"And you think our impatient passenger, if he is our man, is going to quietly stand up and walk with you to a more secluded spot where we can subdue him till help arrives. Right?"

Ted held up his hands. "Okay, okay. I know I'm making it sound simple, but do you have a better idea?"

"I'm worried that Finch might have a gun in his lap and start shooting first, if he feels threatened."

Ted's head jerked back, looking up, considering for the first time, the implications of what Jim was suggesting. "You think he'd just shoot you or me and blow his chances of making it out of the country?"

"Ted, there's just no way of telling how a suspect, desperate to escape will respond to a perceived threat. If confronted, he might choose to fight his way out. Or he might run for it, possibly taking a hostage for insurance. Unfortunately, how he'll behave is totally unpredictable."

Ted sat down and looked hard at Jim. "Or he *might* just give himself up if we both confront him, and he sees it's hopeless."

Jim smiled. "I wish it was that simple. I've seen men who were armed and cornered. They don't often act rationally."

Ted made a face. "So, you don't think it's worth a try then?"

"Not if we make it worse by provoking him to act and one or both of us gets shot in the process."

Ted shook his head impatiently. "So, are we just supposed to sit around and do nothing?"

Jim pushed both his hands down in a placating gesture. "No. No. Of course not, Ted. One of us will keep an eye on Finch. The other one contacts Sergeant Greene on the short-wave radio and bring him up to date on what we know."

"Or how much we don't know, you mean," Ted added sarcastically. The mantle clock chimed once at nine-thirty, interrupting the conversation.

Jim turned slowly to leave the office. "I'll keep an eye on Finch."

Ted raised his hand. "Be…"

Jim caught his hand in mid-air, interrupting, "Careful. I
will. When you get a chance, let me know what's happening
with the station sending some reinforcements."

***

Ted's small workroom was a model of efficient
organization. The ham radio sat in the far corner beside a table
vise and rows of hand tools hanging on a pegboard mounted
against the wall. Ted slipped onto the wooden stool and tuned
the frequency to the police band. "Rutland Police, this is the
Vermont Inn, over." He turned up the volume hearing only
static. He repeated his call. A garbled voice was barely audible
above the static. He fine-tuned the frequency again and
repeated his ID call.

"Ted, this is Sergeant Greene." The sudden clarity and
volume of the voice startled Ted.

"Spencer, I thought I'd bring you up to date."

"Go ahead, Ted."

"We have a person of interest who may be the suspect.
The bus driver got a call from his supervisor warning him
about a possible murder suspect on the bus. We took him into
the office, and he told us about a passenger who seemed highly
agitated that the bus was being diverted. The man's name is
Norman Finch. He's medium height and very angry. He's
currently in the dining room, and we are keeping an eye on
him."

"If you feel you have things under control, I will see
what I can find out about Finch. The power company is still
working on fixing the downed power lines and the DPW is
working on clearing the road between Rutland and the inn. But
given the current whiteout conditions, it'll be at least a couple
of more hours before the highway is open for us to get there. It

looks like the worst of the storm will be over by early morning."

Ted started to ask what Spencer had in mind if they needed backup sooner, checked himself, and looked at his watch. Almost 10:00 pm. If the roads weren't clear enough for them to get to the inn, then the bus wouldn't be going anywhere till around midnight. He wondered aloud how the suspect would take the news of a longer delay. "Spencer, if the suspect *is* here, we're not sure how he'll react to this news. Hell, we don't even know if Finch *is* our suspect."

"Just keep an eye on him. I'll see what I can find out. Under no circumstances should the bus be allowed to leave the inn until we get this sorted out. I don't care if the driver has to make up a story about a frozen gas line or even if he has to sabotage it. Right now, we have some control over the situation with you and Jim there. Keep everyone at the inn."

"Sure Spencer, I'll pull a few ignition wires myself if I have to."

"By the way, any word on the missing owner, Megan King?"

"No. Nothing. If she hasn't found shelter, I don't want to think about her chances of making it through the storm. I hope we can start looking as soon as the storm is over."

Chapter 40

Megan's fitful sleep was jarred by a loud crack outside the playhouse, followed by a slow ripping sound. She bolted upright and was greeted by an explosion of wood and glass showering her with bits of glass, wood, and snow. It took her a moment to realize what had happened. She shook her head and brushed off a fine white powdery coating. Wind and snow whistled through a rough opening filled with broken pieces of green needles and twisted window fragments. Megan swung the billy club wildly at the branches, *Damn, damn, damn you! Why are you doing this to me?* She surveyed the damaged playhouse. She knew she'd have to decide whether to stay there, or risk going out again and try finding her way back to the inn. And she had lost some protection, but at least it was still a refuge from the wind and driving snow. *Maybe that yellow-eyed creature's been frightened off by the noise and won't return to the playhouse.* She made a face. *Given my luck today, what are the chances of that?*

She set about breaking off the longer branches protruding into the playhouse and forcing them back into the opening. *My hands are fucking freezing.* She stood and periodically shook them between her struggles to break the larger branches in two. She collapsed on her makeshift bed and surveyed her handiwork. *Well, I've managed to almost completely fill the hole with broken pine branches.* She got up and stuffed some of the children's old pirate costumes into the remaining spaces. She rocked back and forth; she tucked her fingers into her armpits for warmth.

I think it's time to light two candles and warm another pot of water before my aching hands fall off. She felt for the two warming candles that she had used to make tea a few hours earlier. *Oh shit! Those two candles aren't on the table.* She began feeling the floor with her hands and found the candles under the table partly covered by a thin blanket of snow. *Can anything else go wrong?* She tried to relight them but the wicks on both candles were wet, too wet to light again. On an impulse, she took the comic book from the shelf, muttered an apology under her breath, and tore out the first several pages. Megan twisted the paper into a large wick, lit it, and used the heat from the burning paper to dry the snow-coated wicks on the warming candles. In a few moments, she had both warming candles burning brightly. She collected new snow from the floor of the playhouse, placed the teapot on the stand over the candles and waited for what seemed an eternity for the snow to melt and the water to warm.

Megan held the mug of water, savoring the tingling sensation of warmth against her fingers. She wondered what Bill was doing back at the inn. *Will he tell the staff that she was lost in the woods, or would he be frantically pacing back and forth, unsure what to do?* She sighed. She knew the latter was probably more like Bill. She also knew that was unkind. He'd be worried sick and blaming himself for her being lost. Given the intensity of the storm, it would be impossible to begin any rescue. Any attempt would have to wait till it subsided. *I just hope he doesn't try to find me. He might get disoriented and then we'll both be lost in the woods.*

Megan knew she might not be able to stay the rest of the night in the shelter of the playhouse. *The candles are almost gone. The playhouse won't survive another fallen branch.* She nodded to herself. *Okay. I stay, barring another tree branch damaging the playhouse, I'll hang on till first light before setting out to look for the inn.* She found her makeshift bed of play clothes, picked up her billy club and settled down for what she hoped would be an uneventful night.

In her dream, a small puppy was running through her legs. Young children stood nearby humming a senseless tune that rose and fell in pitch. She smiled, wondering why the frisky ball of fur felt so light. A sudden shiver shook her awake. She looked down to see two mice jumping off her legs onto a shard of broken mug under the table. Megan gave a startled scream reflexively pulling her legs toward her chest, beating the ground with the club. The mice disappeared into two small puffy clouds of white, ringed by a medley of broken green pine needles. *Oh, that was really brave!* Megan had seen hundreds of mice since they moved into the inn. She mostly ignored them unless she saw them in the kitchen or any public areas of the inn.

Megan waited for her pounding heart to subside before deciding to see what other creatures had taken shelter in the playhouse. She slipped off the bench and carefully poked under the table and in the darkened corners of the playhouse. In the corner nearest the door, there was an eruption of snow as a mole darted for the safety of a small knothole near the opposite corner. She checked the cabinets, making sure the catch was securely fastened. Megan decided against trying to get any more sleep. She sat down on the bench and heard a familiar scratching sound outside the door. She glanced down at the club in her hands and realized it would probably be of little use against a hungry wolf. Megan moved cautiously to the door, inspecting the wooden latch, a one-inch wide length of wood about 10 inches long. It was secured to the door on one end and designed to pivot into a U-shaped catch on the door jamb. She moved her fingers along the narrow strip of wood toward the door frame. She felt the wood bow inward as the weight of the snow pressed against the door. Her fingers reached the catch and she realized it was only partially seated and might pop out.

So, do I try to push the latch down more or just sit tight and hope it holds? Almost in answer to her question, there resumed a more persistent scratching on the door. *Okay. I make it more secure.* Megan placed the end of the club against the top edge of the latch and pushed down. It immediately slipped off the latch. She centered the end of the club squarely on the latch and pushed again. It held on the latch, but nothing budged. *It's too tight. I need to pound this latch closed.* She felt around in the dark for something substantial to use to hammer the end of the club. Her fingers found a small cast iron skillet on the floor under the shelf. The cold metal startled her, and she pulled her windbreaker over her fingers to keep her hand from freezing on the metal. She held the club against the latch, raised the skillet and brought it down squarely on the end of the billy club.

There was a dull 'thump' as the small frying pan bounced off the top of the club and into the air, still clutched in her hand. At the same time, the narrow strip of wood, already bending under the pressure of snow against the door splintered with a sharp 'crack.' Megan's startled *Shit* was cut off by a small explosion of snow as the door popped open, knocking her back a step. A startled coyote fell forward through the doorway landing on his face. As he fought to regain his footing in the loose, slippery snow, Megan swung the frying pan down as hard as she could against his head yelling, *Get out of my house!.* The coyote howled in pain as he quickly backed out of the door and fled into the night. Megan laughed in nervous exhaustion mumbling to herself, *Get out of my house? What the hell am I saying? I must be delirious, losing my mind in all this cold.*

She looked at her watch, surprised to see that it was only 10:15. She crawled to the doorway and peered into the darkness. *Is it possible? It seems as though the storm has lessened in intensity. Or maybe it's just a lull before the next band of snow.* Megan knew that the little playhouse didn't have the same protection that it had a few hours earlier. She debated whether to stay put until morning or venture out and try to find her way back to the inn. *I've only been cooped up here for a few hours. Am I just being stupid? Stay or go? Go. It's time to try again.* She pulled on a pair of too small mittens, grabbed the billy club, and crawled slowly on her hands and knees out through the white tunneled opening into the snow-swirled night.

Chapter 41

As Jim went about his job of getting drinks and filling water glasses, he casually surveyed the dining room to see who might be watching him. He had an uneasy feeling someone had been, but he wasn't sure who. There were four tables with one patron each, the rest had anywhere from two to six. The single tables had Finch, one was empty with a half-eaten meal—in the lounge or bathroom maybe, another had an older woman in a stylish two-piece suit with her hair in a bun, and a younger man in his twenties with short hair, jogging pants and a quilted down jacket. Some of the larger tables were mixed groups—couples, singletons, and families. Ted stood at the entrance to the dining room, caught Jim's eye, and then returned to the kitchen. Jim knew he couldn't immediately leave the room without attracting attention. He stayed filling water glasses till his pitcher was empty, then walked out into the kitchen, as if to get more water.

"Okay. what did Spencer say?"

"Looks like the roads won't be clear for a couple of more hours. We need to make sure the bus stays here till we figure out whether the suspect was on this bus."

Jim made a face. "I'm afraid we need to ask John to make an announcement that will make him very unpopular."

"I'll get him from the lounge, so we don't call too much attention to ourselves," Ted offered. He left the sitting room and found John nursing a dark beer at the end of the bar. "John, we need to talk."

John looked up from his foamy-topped reflections, nodded once, and followed Ted into the office.

Ted took a deep breath before speaking. "John, the police have informed us that the driving conditions are still treacherous and need the bus to stay at the inn until they know more about the possible suspect."

John shook his head wearing a sad smile. "The day just keeps getting better and better. And let me guess, you'd like me to let the passengers know they'll be here a little longer."

"I'm sorry, but yes, I would."

"Our friend Mr. Finch is going to blow a gasket when he hears this."

"Jim and I will be close by in case he gets too agitated."

"I wish I could tell you I feel reassured by that, but I don't. No offense, Ted."

They agreed that John would return to the bar by way of the men's room and Ted would stay for a few extra minutes in the office.

Benny returned from Room 21 and slid easily into the captain's chair in front of his half-eaten meal and began deliberately buttering a dill role and observing the other guests dining in the room. *Everyone's busy talking except for my sullen friend. Finch is done with his steak and is trying to catch the eye of any waitress to take it away. They're completely ignoring him.* As Benny finished his meal and took another sip of his coffee, he noticed the handyman who earlier had carried in wood, walk to the entrance to the dining room from the office, look briefly over at the fireplace and then leave through the kitchen. *I wonder if he's checking on more than if the fire needs wood. No one seemed to leave and follow him out of the room.* He nodded to himself, confident that nothing suspicious was going on. He knew that Heidi and Dave might be a more immediate concern. He doubted they'd be missed before morning. They had finished their meal and retired for the evening. With weather conditions being so bad, Benny hoped they didn't have plans to meet anyone else this evening at the inn. He felt confident he could leave them tied up in their room and be out of the country before they were discovered the next morning. As he lifted the cup to drain his last mouthful of coffee, he heard the bus driver's voice asking for attention.

"May I have your attention, please.?" The noise level in the lounge gradually diminished, and Ted suddenly appeared back in the dining room. "I've just received word from the local police that the intensity of the storm is delaying the clearing of the road between here and Route 7. They informed me that it won't be clear for another couple of hours. That means that the earliest we will be leaving the inn is," he squinted at his watch, "around midnight." The hush was replaced by a loud buzz of voices that quickly filled the room.

Benny heard the announcement feeling knives stab the bottom of his stomach. *Shit. A longer delay might greatly complicate my life. All I need is for the bus to still be here at daybreak.* He pictured a screaming maid standing in the doorway, finding Heidi and Dave tied up. Before Benny could think any more about what he might be forced to do, Finch, his face red with anger, rushed into the lounge and began yelling at the driver.

"Do you mean to tell me I have to spend two more hours in this backwater inn?"

John wheeled to face his accuser. His face turned a dull crimson; his hands clenched into tight fists as he fought to control his temper. "Yes Mr. Finch. I do. Do you honestly think I like being stuck here anymore than you?"

"All I know is you *could* drive us to Montreal, but you're afraid of driving in a little snow."

John started to respond, but Ted stepped between them. "Maybe we should discuss this in a quieter place."

Finch glared at Ted. "I don't need a quieter place."

Ted stared hard at Finch as he spoke. "Mr. Finch, I insist. I am going to ask Bill King, the owner, to join us in the sitting room. I am *sure* we can work something out." Ted extended his arm and Finch stood for a moment scowling. Then he turned and stomped out of the lounge, reminding Ted of a spoiled child, used to getting his own way.

Jim had watched the scene from the edge of the dining room, ready to step in if necessary. *I can't hurry over there without raising too many suspicions, if we're wrong about Mr. Finch.* He shook his head. *I have this uneasy feeling that Finch is a bit too vocal and obnoxious to be our man.* He turned and walked back into the kitchen.

Benny pushed back his chair. *That handyman was pretty quick to step in. And then he led Finch off into the sitting room. He seems more than just hired help, What else does he do besides haul wood? Better keep an eye on him. I need to find out what's going on.* Benny threw down enough to cover the check, picked up his briefcase, and walked over to inspect the row of pictures on the wall between the lounge and the sitting room.

Ted tried to get everyone to sit down. He was painfully aware that Finch might have a gun hidden and ready to use. He knew that Jim wasn't there, and he wasn't prepared to deal with that possibility. "Mr. Finch, please sit down." Finch stood, arms crossed in front of him, feet slightly apart, breathing slowly and noisily.

"I am comfortable the way I am."

"I know. But we are not," said Ted, motioning to himself and a seated Bill King and John Doherty. Finch made a disgruntled face, then turned looking behind him, and dropped into a single overstuffed chair facing the sofa. Ted began speaking slowly and deliberately. "Mr. Finch, we are all as anxious to see you get safely to Montreal as you are."

Finch interrupted, "If I miss my connection, it will cost me dearly. I can't *afford* to miss my flight to South America."

Benny smiled to himself. *What a lucky break. I might not even have to buy a ticket to South America.*

"Mr. Finch, I'm monitoring road conditions on my ham radio and promise we'll have you on the road as soon as humanly possible."

So, the handyman has a ham radio. That's another way for this guy to communicate with the outside world. He cocked his head as he considered this idea. *What are the chances? No. That seems just too far-fetched.*

Finch appeared to be making up his mind about something. Ted held his breath and waited. In a low resigned voice, Finch responded, "This sucks. I'm stuck here and I really don't have any choice."

On a hunch, Bill added, "Tell you what Mr. Finch, to help make your stay here less stressful, all your food and drinks are on the house."

Finch, who was looking down, looked up quickly. He hesitated, his eyes weighing the offer and said, "Deal! And I'm suddenly feeling quite thirsty." He stood up with a smug look on his face like he had just pulled a fast one and headed for the lounge. Ted and Bill looked at each other in surprise.

Benny had edged closer to hear the end of their conversation, bumping into a low table under a picture of an old farm that eventually became the Vermont Inn. He swore silently under his breath and massaged his shin. He heard Finch say he was going to get a drink, so he hurried away from the picture and grabbed an empty seat at the end of the bar nearest the window.

He smiled to himself as he considered how preoccupied the staff were with their unruly guest. *You're all right where I want you to be.* He turned to the bartender and ordered a large draft beer as he reached for a newly filled bowl of salted peanuts.

Chapter 42

Megan set off from the playhouse towards what she hoped was the lawn outside of the inn. A few times she thought she passed landmarks that looked familiar, like the rock-filled ravine that in the spring and summer held a rushing stream. She seemed to recall that there was an access road nearby that eventually led to Route 4, the state highway that ran in front of the inn. Her fingers and toes were starting to feel numb. She fought through deep snow up the side of the ravine and pushed through a sentry of barren birch trees.

Megan stopped, her energy gone, taking heaving gulps of icy air, already feeling the steady seductive tug to drop and fall into merciful sleep. She shook her head. *I am not going to sleep. I'm not going to die here in the woods. I will see my family again.* Taking another deep breath, she gritted her teeth, forcing her legs to keep going, one torturous step after another. She tried but failed to ignore the muscles screaming in her legs to stop. She looked up and squinted. *Are my eyes playing tricks on me? It looks like there's a faint light in the middle of that wall of darkness.* Megan stopped and closed her eyes. *Please, let this be the way out.* She opened her eyes. *Whatever that is, it's still there. Thank God.* The brightening intensified as she stumbled on, falling, getting up, pushing the limits of her fatigue with desperate hope. She fought her way through a stand of birch trees, breaking through and then toppling down a small incline into a treeless expanse about thirty feet wide, stretching as far as she could see in either direction.

She stood up, confused, and looked right and left. *Where the hell am I? I'm not near the inn, and this is definitely not Route 4. Then what is this?* She shook her head, looking left then right. *It has to be an access road. But which way leads to the highway?* She took a deep breath looking down. *I'm such*

195

a lousy guesser. She turned to the right. Her legs plowed through drifted waves of endless white, each step sapping any remaining energy and her will to continue. *If I'm wrong, if I'm wrong. Oh shit, I can't be wrong.* Several times she stopped, drawing in deep lungful's of air. After walking for what felt like hours she saw a brightening ahead. *This has to be it. It **has** to be it.* Adrenalin pushed her on. *One more step, just one more step. Each step closer to what?* She reached a six-foot wall of snow and fell forward against it, starting to sob. She looked up, back down, took a breath and started climbing. *One hand, one foot, push, other hand, other foot, push. I just don't have any more energy. But I'm so fucking close.* She closed her eyes and gave a final push. Megan's mittens slipped off as she pulled herself to the top, completely out of breath. *Let me just die here. I'm done.* She rolled over on her back and felt herself tumbling, falling face first down the steep snow bank blocking the unplowed access road.

She landed breathless in a snow-coated heap onto a broad plowed highway...Route 4. She shook her head and sat up in ankle-deep snow feeling an exhausted relief. *This has to be the highway. The inn should be down there, somewhere. Maybe I can walk the rest of the way.* She stood up trembling, barely able to stand. *And maybe not.* She heard a droning sound in the distance behind her and turned around, hoping to flag down the passing motorist. Two lights were swerving toward her less than two hundred feet away. Megan screamed, *Oh shit! No. I am not getting run over!* She turned and tried to run but her legs gave out and she fell heavily. She scrambled to her knees watching her shadow grow larger against the snow bank. She turned, threw her hands up in front of her face screaming, *God. No!*

Chapter 43

Joe woke with a start as the Jeep, buffeted by a fierce wind gust, shuddered violently and bounced sideways jumping out of a solitary plowed corridor of snow and against a drift crested along the side of the highway. Nia swore as she fought the wheel easing the car back into the center of the road. "Where are we?" mumbled Joe as he shook his head and ran his fingers through his unruly gray-flecked hair.

"Well, it's 10:45 and we've been on the road over four hours and I think we're about fifteen minutes away from the Killington Ski Area. The storm seems to letting up a bit, the closer we get." Nia squinted. She tried in vain to pierce the shifting veil of swirling white and knew it could easily take a lot longer to reach the inn. Nia also knew it would be too dangerous to just drive up to the inn. She glanced down at the CB radio mounted beneath the dash. "Does the CB radio work?"

"Everything in Bette works fine," smiled Joe as Nia continued to fight to keep the Jeep under control. "But in these mountains, under these conditions, all you'll get is a lot of static, I'm afraid."

The roads unexpectedly became clear as the jeep approached the Killington ski area access road. Massive snowplows from the ski resort, their lights slicing a blinding swath through the snow, could be seen scouring the asphalt in preparation for the anticipated deluge of ski enthusiasts. Joe and Nia looked at each other and simultaneously said, "the CB!" Joe lifted the handset and said, "Rutland police this is Detective Joe Donovan, over." Seconds of static was following by a crackling voice.

"Detective Donovan? This is Sergeant Spencer Greene. You sound like you are in a cement mixer. How can I help you?"

"Sergeant Greene, I'm traveling with Detective D'Amato on Route 4 approaching Killington. The plows are doing a hell of a job, and the roads up here are passable. What's the situation at the inn?"

"Killington! Well, I'll be damned. I've already dispatched another squad car to the inn. It's just arrived west of there on Route 4 and is waiting on my orders. If your suspect *is* at the inn, we don't want to spook him, but take him quietly. Oh, you should also know, we also have one of the owners, Megan King, missing in the woods somewhere east of the inn. Her current status is unknown. If the roads stay clear, you should be there about eleven-twenty. You'll need to hold your position east on Route 4. You'll know you are close when you see High Ridge Road on your right less than one hundred yards before the inn. It's likely the sign will be buried by snow."

"Right. We'll let you know when we arrive. Donovan out."

They rode for the next fifteen minutes straining to see the access road sign through the snow. Joe and Nia glimpsed the darkened outline in the road at the same time. Nia instinctively hit the brakes and turned the wheel, causing the jeep to swerve sideways and sickeningly slide toward the figure. She eased the wheel in the opposite direction, keeping steady pressure on the brakes and slowly began to regain some traction. The vehicle began to respond, changing direction but not decelerating fast enough. The jeep slid past the trembling, terrified shape, missing it by inches. Joe jumped out of the vehicle before it came to a stop and ran back to the hooded figure now slumped and shaking in the snow.

"Are you alright?"

A small trembling voice sobbed, "I will be."

"What are you doing, walking out on Route 4 in a snowstorm?"

"Lost. I, I got lost in the woods."

"Megan? Are you Megan King?"

For the first time, the woman looked up. Her face was scratched and bruised, but defiant. "Yes."

"My God. There's a lot of folks worried about you. I'm Joe Donovan, a Boston Police Detective." To her startled look he replied, "Yes, it's a long story. But you must be frozen. Let's get you into the car."

Donovan opened the back door to the jeep. "Detective D'Amato, meet Megan, the missing innkeeper."

"Megan, thank God I didn't hit you!" She looked at Joe who was opening up a blanket and putting it around the shivering figure. "And I have some bad news. The jeep is running, but the front end is stuck in a snowbank."

Joe nodded. "Yeah, I noticed. Let's switch places. You call Sergeant Greene and I'll work on getting Bette unstuck."

Nia picked up the mic. "Spencer, this is Nia, over."

"Go ahead, Nia."

"We found Megan! She's here in the car with us warming up."

"That's the first good news I've heard since this snow storm started. How is she?"

Nia glanced in back at the shivering blanket. "All I can tell is she's wet, cold, tired, and bruised. Unfortunately, our jeep got stuck in a snowbank, but Donovan's working to free it." The engine noise rose and fell as Joe gently rocked the car back and forth.

"You two stay with Megan until we can get someone there to help. You can also provide eyes on the ground in case things at the inn go south."

Nia interrupted, "Won't you need more help?"

"Appreciate the offer. But staying put makes things less complicated on our end. Look, I want to get back to Jim and Ted with the good news about Megan. I'll keep you in the loop about what's happening. Out."

Joe could tell by Nia's angry eyes and her half open mouth that she was ready to argue and wasn't about to stay in the Jeep. Nia looked back at Megan huddled under blankets lying on her side in back with her eyes closed. She was exhausted and seemingly not privy to any of the recent events happening at the inn. "Joe, call Spencer back in five minutes and tell him you just couldn't stop me from helping. I headed out to the inn and will stay out of sight unless they need reinforcements."

Joe started to speak, then just shook his head as Nia slipped out of the Jeep and headed to the inn to wait for events to unfold.

Chapter 44

Jim had stayed working in the dining room until Finch appeared, heading for the bar. He walked to the entrance and caught Ted's eye, motioning with his head toward the kitchen. As they passed through the swinging door, Ted started to say, "That went easier than I…"

Jim interrupted him in a grim voice shaking his head saying, "It's not him."

"What?" Ted turned toward him, startled.

"It's not him. Finch is a spoiled blowhard *and* a bully, but he's no murderer." Jim paced by the stand-up freezers as Ted could only watched, perplexed. "I've had the feeling for a while now that someone else has been watching us. But they are very good at it, and I can't figure out who it is."

"If you are right," Ted replied slowly "then whoever it is must feel pretty good at the moment thinking that all of our concerns are focused on Mr. Finch. We need a way to take advantage of that. Our real suspect is going to want to keep an eye on us to make sure he has the upper hand and knows what we are up to. We need a way to watch the reactions of the crowd when one of us comes into the room."

Jim nodded. "Okay. Makes sense. How do we do that unobtrusively?"

"Most of the patrons are either in the bar or still in the dining room. We'll start with the dining room. You go into the dining room with this sugar canister and begin filling up the bowls on the breakfast buffet. I'll give you a few minutes for folks to forget you are there and then I'll come in with more wood for the fire. See if you notice anyone paying too much attention. Okay?"

"I guess my only question is…" Jim stopped with a mock serious look on his face. "Where do I find the sugar?"

The dining room still had about half the passengers from the bus. There seemed to be little interest in Jim slowly filling the sugar bowls in the corner of the dining room. After a few minutes, Ted came in with an armload of split logs. Jim noticed that a few diners looked up disinterestedly but quickly went back to their eating and quiet conversations. As Ted placed the last log on the fire, he glanced casually back at Jim who gave his head a slightly disappointed shake. Jim finished filling the bowls, hoisted the sugar canister, and walked back to the kitchen.

Benny checked his watch. *One last hostage check and a trip to the can and the bus should be ready to leave.* He looked up and flagged the bartender. "Watch my things one last time?" The bartender nodded and he slipped off the stool and left the room.

"Nothing going on in the dining room that I could see," Jim reported. "I think the bar might be a little trickier since it's more congested and I think the two of us turning up together to do some job might look a little too obvious."

"You're right. I can watch some of the folks through the glass window in the swinging door to the kitchen, but I'll miss more than I'll see. Why don't you go over and ask the bartender about putting out some bowls with munchies at each of the tables? He knows we are looking for someone and will do whatever you want. When you are on the far side of the room next to the windows, I'll come out of the kitchen and walk to the dining room. We'll both keep our eyes open and see if we can spot someone a little too interested in what's going on."

Jim nodded and left the kitchen, heading for the bar. The bartender looked up briefly as he approached and said, "What can I do you for, Jim?"

"I think it would be a good idea if I put munchies out on the tables for these stranded folks. Okay?"

"The bartender gave Jim a knowing look and said, "Sure." He reached under the bar and produced a stack of medium wooden bowls. He looked again and swiftly lifted a five-gallon container of munchies onto the bar. "If I'm not careful, I'll find myself out of a job." He smiled and turned to refill another guest's beer at the end of the bar. Jim started filling the bowls and placing them on the tables, noting the reactions of people as he passed. As promised, Ted emerged from the kitchen as Jim finished putting out the snacks at a table near the window. He turned and studied the patrons as Ted walked casually out of the kitchen and into the dining room. Jim waited until they were both back in the kitchen.

Jim's face was etched in disappointed as he spoke. "I don't get it, Ted. Everyone seemed preoccupied either with the folks at their table or their drinks. No behavior seemed out of place. This just doesn't make any sense. I know I'm missing something, but what?" Ted could only shake his head in response.

By the time Benny returned to the bar, Jim had already finished filling the munchie bowls and returned to the kitchen to talk to Ted. Benny checked the time. 11:00 pm. *If I'm lucky, I won't have to visit the couple in Room 21 again as long as they stay quiet. The inn and those two lovebirds will be ancient history by the time I'm out of the country.*

Benny looked outside, noticing that the snow seemed to be lessening in intensity. "Hey, look at that," Benny announced in a clear voice, to no one in particular. "It looks like the snow might be stopping." Benny looked over at Finch slouched over his drink at the other end of the bar. *Well that should stir things up a bit.*

Ted had entered the dining room and was tending the fireplace when he heard the loud pronouncement. He shook his head. "Great. That's just what we need. Finch is going to go ballistic again." He replaced the fireplace poker and headed toward the bar.

Finch, who seemed intent on getting as many free drinks as he could before they left, looked up with glazed eyes, slid precariously off his bar stool, and wobbled over to John, sitting alone at a dining room table. " Hey bus driver. You should be out there warming it up for us. Why are you just sitting there?"

A small crowd began to gather, talking excitedly and pointing at the lessening intensity of the storm. John stood up grim-faced, as Finch approached, trying unsuccessfully not to show his anger. Ted rushed over.

"Mr. Finch, we know the storm is lessening in intensity. We are just checking to make sure the roads are open and safe before you leave. I am sure you'll be on your way before midnight."

Finch twisted his face in a failed attempt at disbelief. He snorted, "Well in that case, I think I may have time for just one more drink."

As Finch staggered away, Ted noticed a man watching the entire episode intently from the bar with a slight smile playing on his lips. He thought this odd behavior for someone who should be anxious to leave and get to Montreal. He didn't remember seeing him earlier when they were monitoring the passenger's reactions after dinner. It would seem this guy had an odd habit of disappearing. Ted returned to the kitchen where he was immediately intercepted by Jim.

"Are you crazy? On their way *before* midnight? And if it doesn't happen, *then* what are we going to do?"

Ted nodded. "Okay." He took a deep breath. "I know. I spoke too soon. The words were out before I realized what I was saying. But, I *did* learn something interesting. There was a man sitting at the bar, who seemed to be monitoring the whole scene with a little smile. When he noticed me looking, he looked quickly away. It might be nothing, but this is exactly the kind of thing we've been looking for. This guy seems to fit what we know about the suspect." Ted stopped momentarily. "And he does seem to be missing whenever we go out to monitor everyone's reaction."

"What does he look like, so I know who I'm looking for?"

Ted started counting on his fingers. "Well first, he fits what we know already: male, middle-aged, average build, about six feet, with dark eyes. And this guy has a ponytail and he's wearing a blue Patriot's jacket."

"Well, that will make it easy to keep tabs on him. Why don't we find out the status of reinforcements and the roads out of here from Spencer?" Jim pointed toward the kitchen's back door.

Ted shook off the snow, then walked over to his work bench and picked up the handset. As he opened his mouth, the speaker crackled to life with Spencer's voice.

"Ted, this is Spencer, over."

"Just ready to call you, Spencer. Go ahead, I'm here with Jim."

"I've got two men who are waiting in a squad car just west of Cream Hill Rd. on Route 4 awaiting orders. We also have the additional support of two officers just east of the inn on Route 4. Oh, when you have a chance, tell Bill that Megan has been found and she is okay."

"Thank God! That's great news!"

"What's the situation on your end?"

"We have ruled out Finch as our suspect. He's volatile, but Jim doesn't see him as someone who could pull this off. I have reason to believe it may be another man. He's about six feet, olive complexion, ponytail, and about 175 pounds. He's smart enough not to draw attention but is watching Jim, and I like a hawk and I have a hunch he knows how to stir up trouble without getting involved. I wish we had more to go on. I don't want to grab the wrong guy while the suspect gets away."

"I think our best strategy is to try to stall the bus leaving while my two officers make their way to the inn. It shouldn't be more than 15 minutes. You keep an eye on ponytail in case he is our suspect and apprehend him if he makes any sudden moves. Jim, you meet the two officers at the entrance, and bring them in to confront the suspect." He added, "Oh, and there's a friend of yours outside the inn in case we need backup."

"Friend? What friend?"

"Detective Nia D'Amato, your old partner. She found out you were in the middle of this and drove up from Boston to help ID your suspect."

"D'Amato. Well, I'll be dammed. She's one of the smartest cops I ever worked with. Excepting you, of course," he added quickly.

"Excepting me, of course. So, I think we have a plan that we all agree."

Jim interrupted, "Hold on Spencer. I see some flaws in that plan. There are too many things that can go wrong. The suspect may not be on the bus at all, and we scare some poor guy half to death. I know—no harm was done. *Or* he could be on the bus and is better at keeping a low profile. So, he just watches us make fools of ourselves. Then again, it could be this ponytail character who decides to go rogue and take matters into his own hands when confronted or when he senses things getting out of control."

"If you have a better idea, I'm open to suggestions. The best plan will be the one that works, with nobody getting hurt. But we just can't know that up front."

"How about this. We'll ask the passengers to file out to the bus one at a time because of the ice and snow, for *safety* reasons. We need to get this guy by himself so that if he decides to start making trouble, we can minimize the risk to the passengers and end it quickly. While I'm not positive this guy is our perp, I think it's a better option given what we know."

Jim imagined seeing Spencer nodding as he agreed to go along with his plan. They worked out the details of who would be positioned inside and outside the inn. They agreed that Ted should help the passengers get into single file as they left the lobby. Jim would be stationed at the door, staggering their exit, ready to signal two officers waiting unseen outside the door to confront their suspect when he walked to the bus. His reaction to their approach would dictate what they did next.

Chapter 45

Heidi looked at Dave, unconscious, softly moaning, and tied against the bedpost. She knew they were at the mercy of their assailant who might return at any time to rape, torture, kill her and certainly Dave. She tested the strips of terry cloth holding her hands and legs. The knots were secure, and there was no slack in the material. Her limbs ached from being tightly stretched, and she realized how totally vulnerable she was. She heard Dave starting to stir, still leaning heavily against the belt holding him to the bedpost. She started rocking the bed so that the headboard hit the wall. Every motion forward and backward produced waves of pain as the terry cloth dug into her wrists. Beads of sweat rolled down her forehead stinging her eyes. Her breathing became shallow and ragged. She glanced down at Dave as he bobbed forward and back as the headboard tapped the wall in gentle, steady rhythm. She prayed someone would notice.

An older couple, returning to their room after dinner, had stopped just outside Heidi and Dave's room.

The husband turned to the wife. "Why are we stopping here, dear?"

"Don't you hear that? Do you think there might be a problem?

He stopped and cocked his head listening. A slow smile spread across his face. "Let me think. There's the gentle sounds of a banging headboard. And moaning. Has it really been that long, honey?" He shook his head, looking at her with a knowing grin.

She looked at him confused, then dawning realization spread across her face. "Oh, dear." Her face blushed a faint pink. She took his hand. "Let's give that nice couple some privacy." They both walked away smiling at long ago memories.

***

Benny glanced at his foam-topped glass and then up at the bartender. "I thought I was done, but nature calls again. I'll be right back. Watch my briefcase again, okay?"

"Sure."

Benny never made it to the bathroom. He froze as the PA system crackled to life. "Could I have your attention, please?" There was a pause. "The bus will begin boarding in about twenty minutes. To ensure everyone's safety, we will line up single file as we make our way out of the lobby and board the bus. We ask that you move carefully since it's slippery and give each person some extra room. Thank you for your cooperation."

Benny frowned, looking at his watch. *It's 11:20. We're leaving earlier than I thought. That's good news. But leave extra room and walk single file. I don't like the sound of that. I have to come up with a plan to disrupt this single file business.* He turned and slowly walked back to the bar.

It might be risky, but I need to find out more about that unfinished gas fireplace. I seem to remember hearing a news report on a house that exploded because of a propane gas leak near the fireplace in the living room. They talked about how gas is heavier than air and tends to pool at the lowest point. When the owner got home, he apparently smelled gas and turned on the lights to investigate. The tiny spark from the light switch caused a massive explosion, killing the owner. What a dumb shit. He considered this new possibility as he slipped back onto his bar stool.

"Another beer, sir?"

He had been so absorbed in his problem that he didn't notice he had almost finished his beer. He smiled as he looked up, "I think I may have just enough time to finish this one."

Benny held up his hand to attract the bartender's attention again. "So, do most of these places use natural or propane gas?"

The bartender turned away from wiping out some of the munchie bowls. "All of the places around here use bottled gas. We have a big one out in back. Why?"

"I read in your brochure that some rooms will have gas fireplaces. That's a great idea for an inn here in Vermont. I just wondered what they used."

The bartender nodded in agreement. "And that's one of the things that bring people back here. Besides the food and drink, of course", he added with a wink."

"If I decide to come back again and stay, do you have any idea when the fireplaces will be ready to go?"

"Oh, I think Ted said he mostly has everything hooked up—gas, electricity, and exhaust. He just needs to add the insert and then finish adding the decorative trim." He stopped for a moment and looked up at the ceiling. "You know, Ted works pretty quickly. I'll bet they'll be up and running before the end of this week."

"That's just, perfect!" Benny replied with a slight smile.

"Hey, are you a fan of the Patriots,?" he asked pointing at Benny's jacket.

Benny looked down, remembering he was still wearing the Patriots jacket he took from the dying Will Caulder back in Boston. "Yes I am. And they are having a good year. Brady's a hell of a quarterback. Maybe they'll go all the way to the Super Bowl."

"Wouldn't surprise me," remarked the bartender as he moved away to offer a refill to another patron at the bar.

Benny lifted his beer, watching the foam slide down the glass. *Wow. I really do need to take a piss.* He looked around and saw the place was alive with a drowsy hum of conversation. *Perfect.* He grabbed his briefcase, slipped off his stool, and made his way to the bathroom in the corridor next to the office. He felt increasingly confident that his identity was safe. They would be on their way to Canada soon and with any luck, he'd have another ticket and ID, courtesy of Finch. He washed his hands, feeling his troubles would soon be spiraling down the drain like so many frothy bubbles. He left the bathroom and started down the corridor toward the bar and stopped. *I think it's time to pay a final visit to my hostages.* He sauntered up the stairs, hearing a gentle tapping sound that seemed out of place. It got louder as he walked past the first two rooms, stopping at room 21. There was no doubt where the sound was coming from.

He slid into the room. Heidi froze in mid-stroke. "I thought I could have one drink before I came back to check on you. But I guess not." Benny grabbed the headboard, raised his foot, and kicked Heidi in the ribs. He glanced over at Dave and saw him glaring in his direction straining heavily against his terrycloth ropes. Heidi gasped from the pain as blood oozed from the corner of her mouth dribbling down her chin. He bent down and examined Dave's bound hands and legs. "Wow! You've been a busy boy." He re-tightened the knots.

He checked his watch. It was 11:30. *Not too soon to start things in motion if they start lining up in a few minutes.* "Dave, I think tonight might be a perfect evening for a little fire." Dave's face bulged with the effort to break free as a torrent of unrecognizable sounds issued from his mouth. "I think you're swearing at me, Dave. Not nice." Benny took out his gun and swung it hard against the side of Dave's head. Dave's head rebounded from the blow causing his eyes to roll up into his head. Heidi's eyes shot open and she gave a muffled scream through the terry cloth stuffed into her mouth. Benny looked over, shook his head, then grabbed a discarded sweatshirt from a nearby chair and placed it roughly over her head. "You sure know how to make a lot of noise. I think this will make it easier on both of us."

"All I need," he looked around the room, "is that." He pointed to the candle on the night table. He gave a half smile as he lifted the jar and left the room saying, "Enjoy the rest of your unforgettable evening, Heidi." He heard her loud throaty grunts fade to silence as he closed the door and walked into the room next door.

He headed directly to the bathroom and placed the candle inside the shower up on the soap shelf to the right of the showerhead. It took several strikes for the match to light. When it finally burst into flame, he lit the wick with a flourish and tossed the match over his shoulder. He smiled grimly as he strode back into the room heading for the hole in the wall that would hold the fireplace. He reached in and pulled the flexible yellow gas connector forward. He rocked the plastic plug back and forth out of the valve at the end of the connector. Then he grabbed the red valve handle and twisted it ninety degrees. A deadly ominous hissing sound filled the room. *Mission accomplished.*

As Benny left the room and descended the stairs to the lobby, he felt a familiar jab of panic stab the pit of his stomach. He hadn't considered how long it would take for the gas, now rapidly flooding the room, to reach the candle in the shower. He was sure the explosion, whenever it did happen, would be terrific. He was equally sure he did not want to be anywhere near the inn when it did happen.

He stopped in the sitting room and dropped on the sofa. His intuition, which had saved him so often in the past, was setting off alarm bells. Benny started absentmindedly leafing through the scrapbook on the coffee table. *Do they know?* He got up and sauntered toward the bar. As he slid onto a bar stool, he caught the handyman glance over his way from the dining room. *I think the handyman may be watching me. He knows or suspects something.* The handyman left the dining room and returned to the kitchen. *I need to avoid him and get out of here as soon as I can. The safest place for me to spend the next few minutes is somewhere out of sight.* He had just entered the bathroom when he heard John make an announcement that they would start boarding shortly, and everyone should make their way to the lobby and line up. *Someone has to smell the gas before it explodes. I need some chaos out there to distract attention before we start boarding.*

Just then the bathroom door opened, and Finch stood unsteadily, trying to keep his balance, reaching out and leaning heavily against the door jamb. He looked up and attempted to smile at Benny, his mouth twisting into more of a smirk. "Zup." He edged hand over hand leaning on the wall to the first urinal and clumsily fumbled for the zipper to his pants. Benny looked over and smiled at the struggling drunken face. *You'll be lucky to find it you pathetic, drunk bastard. But you'll never know how happy I am to see you.* Finch's face sagged in confusion as he looked at the gun sitting in Benny's hand.

Chapter 46

Nia slowly trekked along Route 4, slipping and falling to her knees twice, before she reached the road to the inn. She spotted a squad car by the side of the road less than a hundred yards away and debated whether to lose time introducing herself or move into position closer to the inn. *Guess I'm going to ignore protocol again.* She headed up the access road, using the small lighted spruce trees lining the entryway as a guide. She crouched low and moved forward, taking up position behind one of the snow piles ringing the far edge of the parking lot. *I wonder what the two officers will make of a lone figure walking up the road to the inn. I'm sure Joe will have called Spencer by now and the two officers already know or will know shortly.* Ahead she dimly saw the outline of a bus piled high with snow. She stopped on the driver's side, knowing she was breaking another rule and waited for signs of activity. She settled into a make-shift pocket of snow and glanced at her watch. It was almost 11:40. Her thoughts turned to her old partner, Jim and the occasion when he saved her life.

***

It was a routine domestic disturbance call. Neighbors reported angry shouting and sounds of things breaking coming from a small end unit on Garfield Ave. in one of Hyde Park's housing projects. Nia followed department protocol, one officer knocking on the door, announcing their presence while the second officer stood back and off to one side. The shouting inside suddenly stopped. The door was wrenched opened quickly revealing a large man of Hispanic descent, his face flushed, in a Boston Red Sox t-shirt and loose lounge pants. He held nothing in his hands and spoke in an even steady voice

214

with only a hint of an accent. "Yes, officer. What seems to be the problem?"

She told the man that the station had received calls of a domestic disturbance and they were there to investigate. In the background, she could see a woman sitting on a sofa with her face in her hands surrounded by an assortment of objects on the floor.

He politely replied, "Officer, I assure you, it was only a lover's quarrel. We had a disagreement over my spending too much on lottery tickets. There is no cause for alarm."

Nia looked at him nodding and eyed the terrified look on the lady sitting on the sofa. She told him they would like to come in and just check to make sure the young lady was okay.

The man's face morphed into an angry mask as he pulled a small caliber gun out of his pocket shouting, "No. Puerco! You can't come in and check on the lady. You can die!"

Nia took a stumbling step backward, startled. She started to reach for her gun, knowing it wouldn't be in time. The deadly concussive sound of a gun firing sent her diving to one side, believing it would be the last thing she would ever hear. Looking up she saw the man in the doorway stumbling backward with a neat red-tinged hole in his forehead. Jim's grim face stared wide-eyed, his breathing steady, with his drawn gun held tightly in both hands.

***

After briefing John on what to say over the PA system, Ted and Jim split up. Jim left to stand outside the door to the inn and wait for the two backup officers. After making the announcement, John walked out of the lobby, over to the bus, opened the door, and started the engine. Passengers already beginning to leave the restaurant and bar and gather in the foyer. Ted helped them line up, remembering he hadn't seen Bill to tell him about Megan. He scanned the crowd looking for Benny so that he could keep an eye on him. As Ted turned back to check the empty dining room, he realized he hadn't seen the man with the ponytail since before the announcement. He stopped and took a deep breath. His face turned grim. An unmistakable odor of gas was starting to flood the foyer. He dashed into the kitchen and yelled, "Gas leak. Everybody out the back now!" He raced back through the dining room into the bar yelling, "Change of plan. We need everyone to exit immediately!" He kept repeating the message as he exited the lobby almost knocking down Jim in the doorway and the two officers waiting just outside. "There's a gas leak somewhere inside. We need to get everyone out, now! *And* there's no sign of our suspect."

Finch slumped half-conscious against the urinal opposite the toilet in the lobby bathroom. He stared disbelieving at the man standing by the sink, holding a gun. Benny took one quick step toward Finch, raised the gun high, and brought the handle down hard against his head. Finch grunted as he sagged to the floor spraying urine in an arc across the wall. Benny jumped back quickly to avoid the stream, then stripped off his gray and red winter parker and dragged him into the single stall, wedging him between the toilet and wall, pushing up his feet inside. He took out his Swiss army knife and used the scissors to cut off his ponytail close to his head. He threw the half-foot-long strands at the hunched, unconscious body. Benny removed his Patriot's jacket and gun, then put on Finch's winter jacket, pushing the gun deep out of sight. He tossed his Patriot's jacket over Finch and closed the stall door. He smiled as he found a large knitted hat shoved deep inside one of the pockets. "And this will complete the disguise perfectly."

Benny heard voices shouting from out in the lobby. "Sounds like they know there's a gas leak." He slowly opened the door and saw confused passengers rushing to leave the inn. Benny exited the men's room, ponytail gone, wearing Finch's coat, clutching the briefcase in his left hand and his right hand pressed against the bump in his jacket pocket. He kept the hat low on his forehead so that no one would notice and mixed in with the line of passengers pressing to leave and make their way to the idling bus. As he boarded the bus, he planned to make his way to the back, but changed his mind at the last minute and sat behind the driver with his face turned toward the window, propped by his raised arm as if he were already asleep.

Chapter 47

Sitting in the snowbank, Nia's legs were getting colder and wetter by the minute. *That was a smart move. Charging out here to help has left me cut off from whatever is being planned. In the end, I'll be no help. How long should I sit here before I just go and try to help?* She noticed movement to her left. Two officers walked cautiously up the edge of the drive. A moment later her former partner Jim came out and spoke briefly to them. Nia had started to rise and wave to Jim when he turned and went back inside. The officers appeared to be positioning themselves so they wouldn't be seen.

A minute later, a tall figure came running out shouting something about a gas leak and a change of plan. *A gas leak? It couldn't be a coincidence. It had to be a diversion.* Passengers started streaming out of the inn and climbing into the bus. The two police officers waiting outside were momentarily unsure what to do. *I want to rush in to help, but my gut tells me I should stay here.* Then she noticed, just over the top of the snowbank, a face in one of the first windows on her side of the bus. *It's hard to be sure with that big hat covering the top of his head but it looks like...*

Nia carefully backed out of the snowbank, still hidden from view and made her way several feet along the edge of the parking lot, climbed over a snowbank, and came out in front of the bus. *The two officers have disappeared. They must have decided to lend a hand helping get guests out of the inn.* She waited a moment, then inserted herself into the queue waiting to board the bus. She made her way to the back and sat down. *If I'm mistaken, I'll look like a complete idiot and not for the first time.*

Jim had finished getting all of the guests out of the dining room and bar. He nearly collided with Ted who had quickly checked the bathroom and sitting room and was now headed for the guest rooms above the dining room. They tore up the stairs, the smell of gas overpowering, and started pounding on doors yelling for folks to get out immediately. Most of the guests had already fled, their doors still open, but an elderly couple near the end of the hallway, opened their door looking confused.

Ted yelled, "There's a gas leak! Get out immediately. The couple shuffled past Ted and Jim in their pajamas and disappeared down the stairs. Ted reached room 21 first and pounded on the door and heard muffled sounds from inside. He kicked open the door and stopped, taking in the scene of Heidi tied on the bed and Dave unconscious sitting on the floor. He pulled his utility knife from the case beneath his pant leg and cut through the terry cloth tie binding Heidi's hands and feet. She whispered, "I can't feel my legs. I don't think I can walk."

Jim came into the room and lifted her off the bed, carrying her out the door. Ted worked cutting through Dave's bindings. He tried to pick up Dave but found his dead weight too much. He grasped both of Dave's hands and started pulling, dragging him slowly from the room. As he neared the door he looked behind him hollering, "I could use a little help here!"

Bill heard his shouts and bounded up the stairs. Together they lifted Dave and carried him downstairs. Two police officers took over and carried him out of the inn. They gently lowered him to the ground next to Heidi. She rocked slowly, holding Dave's bloody head, sobbing and gulping air.

Bill turned to Ted. "I think we got everyone else out, I'm going to do one last sweep through the dining room and kitchen." He pointed to the door. "Make sure no one outside is near the inn." Ted turned and raced outside. Many of the guests standing in the parking lot were still near the door in their nightclothes. Ted started swinging his arms, exclaiming in a loud voice, "I need you all to move away from the front of the inn."

Several passengers on the bus were starting to ask when they were going to leave. John hesitated. This was not part of the plan they had discussed. But the last thing he needed was for Mr. Finch to start yelling again. "Yes. Well, I just need to check my passenger list and then do a head count to make sure we are all here." Benny, sitting feet away from the driver realized that they would be one short. He took out his gun, ready to force the driver to leave. John deliberately took his time as he started counting heads. "Thirty, thirty-one, thirty-two, thirty-three, (a slight hesitation), thirty-four. I guess we are all here."

Benny startled. *Thirty-four? No fucking way. There can't be thirty-four. I left Finch unconscious back on the bathroom floor. Had the driver miscounted?* He shook his head. *Unlikely.* He puzzled over who else could have taken Finch's place on the bus? John was clearly uncomfortable leaving the inn in the middle of a crisis that interrupted their careful plans. But he knew it wouldn't be long before Finch, who he suddenly realized was now sitting directly behind him, awoke from his drunken stupor and started yelling, demanding they leave immediately. Reluctantly he closed the doors which came together with a soft hiss. He released the air brake and started the bus slowly moving across the parking lot away from the inn.

Jim heard the snow crunching under the tires. He looked up and saw the bus rolling toward the entrance. "Hey, wait a minute. That's not the plan," he yelled. He started to give chase.

Bill hurried out of the inn, coming up behind Ted. "I didn't find anyone else…"

An ear-splitting explosion and fiery blast threw the two of them to the ground, as glass, wood, and burning particles rained down. The departing Greyhound rocked from side to side. John instinctively slammed on the brakes causing the bus to skid to a stop. A heartbeat passed. Benny leaped up out of his seat and took a step toward John, pointing his gun snarling, "Don't stop. Keep driving." Some of the passengers nearby started yelling in alarm. Benny swung the gun around and started to say, "Shut up." As his weapon swung toward the center aisle of the bus, he faced a familiar figure standing facing him from the back of the bus...Detective Nia D'Amato.

Nia raised her gun. 'It's over. Drop it, Benny." A slight smile played on his lips. He fired once, driving her back against the rear emergency door. The shock of the bullet hitting her shoulder caused Nia to shoot involuntarily. The shot went wide missing Benny. Screaming passengers took cover behind the seats. Nia sat on the floor dazed, still holding her service revolver pointed at Benny. John, his foot still on the brake, reflexively opened the door when the first shot was fired. Benny hesitated, then grabbed his briefcase, turned and jumped down the stairs, leaping off the bus.

Jim was pushed forward by the force of the blast, slamming him to the ground. He looked up as the bus skidded to a stop. It was followed by the sound of two gunshots. He pulled out his gun and started to push himself up on his knees. A man jumped off the bus, a briefcase in one hand, gun in the other. He turned seeing Jim's weapon and fired at the figure kneeling on the ground. Jim toppled over backward, the bullet creasing his scalp. Benny, his face a frozen mask of anger, started walking towards Jim, his gun aimed and ready to fire again. From behind, Nia breathed his name in an angry whisper. Benny spun around. Nia shot once with deadly accuracy, lifting him off his feet and sending him sprawling into the snow. The briefcase flew out of hand and popped open sending neat stacks of money swirling around the motionless figure.

Nia staggered over to the body and felt the neck. No pulse. She walked half bent over to Jim still lying in the snow. Jim looked up, eyes wide, thinking he'd never seen a sight as welcome as his old partner. In a voice tinged with pain, she whispered, "You okay?"

Jim managed a half smile, gingerly touching the side of his head. "I think so. I'm just glad you showed up when you did. Looks like we're both lucky he was a lousy shot."

She knelt beside him responding, "Yeah. Lucky. You could say that. And I'm returning the favor, Walden." He reached out and gave her a hug. She mumbled, "You're probably bleeding all over me." She heard a muffled snort in reply.

Back in the Jeep, Donovan had just glanced into the back seat where Megan was still sleeping soundly when there was a white flash followed by a percussive, "Boom!". A shower of wood and glass rained down in front of them onto Route 4. Megan startled awake. "What....What was that?".

Donovan stared disbelieving. "Trouble!" He had already managed to free the car from the drift, rocking it back and forth. He started moving toward Cream Hill road, wincing as he listened to the car crunch over the fallen debris. Megan's face was pressed against the side window, mouth open, a look of disbelief on her face. He turned onto Cream Hill Road stopping at the entrance. Gun shots suddenly rang out. He turned to Megan, "Stay here!" Donovan pulled a gun out of his ankle holster and jumped out of the car. He slipped, almost falling on the packed snow as he raced toward the inn. He reached the bus and stopped short, surveying the death and destruction. Behind him, he heard a faint sob and a whispered ragged voice.

"Oh my God. Bill!" Megan stumbled past.

Bill sat hunched over on the ground, covered in ashes and bits of glass. He looked down shaking his head, tears streaming down his face. Gone. All gone. Everything's gone. I've lost Megan, and now, I've lost the inn too." Megan walked up behind him.

She touched his shoulder. "Not everything, love," she sobbed. He looked up, scrambling to his feet. They said nothing, but held each other for a long time, tears falling silently onto the dirty blood-stained snow.

Chapter 48

Nia sat fidgeting with the edge of the pillow case, her other arm immobilized by a white sling tied around her neck. *Benny. It was that fucking weasel Benny. He double crossed Will Caulder then double-crossed Vitelli. He must have been feeling pretty good for a while about getting away with the money and the jewels.* She looked down at her sling. *It was stupid of me getting shot.* She knew the rule. Shoot first, ask questions later. *And I know I'm going to catch hell about it. Flynn will be pissed at me taking off to go to Vermont. He knows better than to buy my cover story that my only intention was to visit Jim Walden and I got caught up in events at the inn.*

The phone next to the bed jumped to life, startling her. It was Deputy Commander Flynn.

"Good morning Detective D'Amato."

"Good morning sir."

The Commander's gravelly voice was edged with irritation. "And how are you *feeling* this morning?"

Shit, I recognize that tone of voice. "Well sir, my shoulder's been patched up and at the moment they have my arm in a sling."

"I'm happy to hear you're okay. But, I am *not* happy about you getting involved in a shooting in Vermont. His last sentence was almost shouted into the phone. "Would you like to explain to me exactly how that happened?"

Okay. Definitely not happy. Time for me to eat humble pie. And I cannot lose my temper. "Yes, sir. First, what happened in Vermont was completely unintentional. When I found out our potential suspect might be fleeing the country through Vermont, I thought I'd alert my old partner. And then, well, I thought since I had a couple of days off, I'd go up and visit him and, well, one thing led to another." Her voice trailed off. *What's the worst he could do? Would he suspend me?*

"Detective D'Amato. I *cannot* have you running off chasing suspects who leave our jurisdiction. Do you understand?"

"Well, yes sir. I know that sir." *Don't get angry. He's just looking for some sort of an apology.* "I know I was completely out of our jurisdiction and I should have avoided getting mixed up in the shooting at the inn."

"Sergeant Greene has filled me in on the shooting and retired detective Donovan confirmed that you were planning to visit Jim Walden and just got caught up in the shooting. So let me get this straight. First, you almost ran over the innkeeper, Megan King who was missing, on the way to visit Jim Walden. And then, because your car was stuck in a snowbank, you walked down to the inn where the police were waiting to apprehend and question our suspect."

"Sir, you have to understand, I was worried about my old partner when I found out he was going to..."

"Detective D'Amato. I'm not finished yet. You then got involved in a shootout on a bus with the suspect. According to Sergeant Greene, he was attempting to flee the inn after he set off a gas leak and subsequent explosion designed to divert attention away from identifying him. But neither you nor I believe in all those coincidences, do we, Detective D'Amato?"

I can tell where this conversation is going. What about the good things that came out of my being there? Keep it together, D'Amato. Nia looked up at the ceiling, grimacing, replying in a small voice. "No, sir."

"While I don't discount the fact that you saved two people, one of them a police officer, while almost getting yourself killed, we will discuss any further disciplinary actions when you return. After you are discharged from the hospital, I expect you to report to *our* doctor to evaluate your medical status and your ability to return to work. Oh, and the Department Psychologist, Dr. Young called and left a message that you have an appointment to see her on Thursday." *Shit, I forgot about that appointment. And the Captain hasn't changed a bit. Damn with faint praise, and then keep the sword poised over my head until I get back. What an ass. Suck it up, D'Amato.*

"Yes, sir. Thank you sir." She made a face and clicked off the phone.

Nia was still staring at it when she heard a familiar voice in the doorway. She looked up at Donovan, smiling, leaning on the door jam. "You know, it could have been a lot worse."

Nia made a face. "You should have heard what I was thinking about him the whole time he was talking."

He smiled and nodded sympathetically. "I can just imagine. Sergeant Greene and I did our best to explain how you came to be at the inn, first finding Megan standing in the road, then later saving your old partner by killing Benny."

"I almost forgot about Jim. How is he doing?"

"He went back to work today. He's got a little crease right about here." He pointed to the side of his head. "I think he's doing fine." He'd like you to stop by the house to see the family before heading back to the city. As for the Vermont Inn, I'm afraid it's a total loss, between the initial explosion and the fire that gutted most of the rooms. But Bill and Megan are already talking about plans to rebuild it, hopefully starting in the Spring."

Nia nodded. "Good for them. Did everybody make it out of the inn okay?"

Joe shook his head. "There was one casualty. Norman Finch. Funny thing was, he was found in a stall in a bathroom off the dining room. And there was a length of ponytail and a Patriot's jacket thrown on top of him. He had suffered a concession from a blow to the head, but he actually died from smoke inhalation."

Nia took a breath looking grim. "I'll bet that was Benny's work. Last time I remember, he had a ponytail. I'll bet he cut if off and switched jackets to make it harder to ID him."

A doctor appeared next to Joe. "Miss D'Amato, I just wanted to update you on your injury."

Joe nodded. "Sure. I'll just wait outside."

Nia raised her hand. "No, stay please."

Joe shrugged. "Okay, if you insist."

The doctor opened a page on his clipboard. "You were extraordinarily lucky that the bullet passed through your deltoid muscles, causing just minor soft tissue and some nerve damage. Although it will take some time and physical therapy to regain strength and flexibility in the shoulder, I'd say you should be able to make a full recovery from your injury."

"Well, I've already stayed here overnight. When will I be able to leave?"

The doctor cocked his head. "If you're feeling up to it, I'd say we can discharge you anytime you're ready."

Nia slid quickly off the bed. As her feet hit the floor, she stopped and grimaced as her arm bounced. "Well that was stupid. I still have to get used to this thing." She motioned with her head to her arm in the sling. "Say no more doctor. I'm ready already."

Joe smiled and shook his head. "Glad to see getting shot hasn't dampened your enthusiasm. How about we visit your old partner first, and then head back to the city?"

"Hey, it all sounds good to me. Let's go get Bette who I hope hasn't suffered from her brief encounter with a snowbank."

"Bette is doing just fine. Although I know she's looking forward to a little peace and quiet after the trauma of this trip.

Nia nodded. "Joe, with this banged up shoulder, I guess I'd better ride shotgun, at least for the first part of the trip."

Joe laughed and shook his head. "You know, you almost make me sad I decided to retire."

"Well Joe, I have a feeling our paths just might cross again."

Joe smiled. "And I hope my heart can take all the excitement." Nia laughed as she exited the hospital lobby.

The End

Lightning Source UK Ltd.
Milton Keynes UK
UKHW020708020122
396454UK00008B/1995